# Good Intentions

## The Amish Lantern Mystery Series
## Book 4

### By Mary B. Barbee

Editing Team: Molly Misko, and Jenny Raith

Cover design by Daniela Colleo of www.stunningbookcovers.com/

www.marybbarbee.com

For my mother, who taught me that life should be led with good intentions.

"God save us from people who mean well."

Vikram Seth

# Chapter One

S ophia Adams leaned forward and handed the driver a crisp ten-dollar bill. "Thank you so much for the ride," she said as she opened her door and stepped out onto the dirt. The Amish Inn stretched above her, blocking the early morning sun from view.

The door of the trunk popped open, and the driver jumped out of the car to help Sophia with her bags. "Good luck, Ms. Adams," he said. "And be sure to lock your doors," he said with a wink.

Sophia chuckled and waved her hand in the air, "Oh, don't be silly. I'll be fine. This certainly looks like a safe enough place." She gestured toward the stately bed-and-breakfast in front of her. The inn was a refurbished old quaint house. The wood siding, the shutters and the front porch all had fresh new paint. It almost looked picture perfect, she thought, and she was reminded of why she was there. Lifting her Nikon D3500 camera that dangled from a strap around her neck, she captured a photograph of her first impression of the Amish Inn.

"I'm just sayin'" the driver continued, "there have been some pretty bad things happenin' out here in Little Valley the past few months."

Sophia smiled at him politely. "Yes, I've heard a little bit about that." She grabbed the smaller of the two suitcases and started to make her way up the front steps. The driver quickly grabbed the larger suitcase and followed her, setting it down just outside the front door. He nodded his head, tipped his cowboy hat and Sophia watched as he trotted back down the stairs and backed his car out of the parking space, heading back the way they came.

She took a quick breath. Her stomach was fluttering, a familiar feeling to her. A new assignment in a new town was always so exciting, and after all her research, she was exceptionally excited to visit Little Valley. She reached up to grab the doorknob of the storm door, but before she could make contact, the heavy front door swung open.

Standing there, she was greeted by a gentleman wearing matching plain dark pants and a white button-down shirt. A straw broad-brimmed hat sat firmly on his head.

Sophia concluded instantly that the young man standing before her was Amish. Sophia opened the screen door wide. "*Gute mariye*," she said with a warm smile. The young man looked surprised, nodded and looked away, returning the same greeting with a soft-spoken voice. He reached down and grabbed Sophia's suitcases as he leaned against the storm door, holding it open.

"Welcome," the young man said, stepping aside to let Sophia pass.

"*Denki*. My name is Sophia Adams." Sophia took a few steps forward and stopped. She was immediately mesmerized by the front living area of the inn. "Wow, this is fantastic!" Then remembering her manners, she asked, "What is your name, may I ask?"

"Jonah Troyer. I am the maintenance man here. I heard your car and thought I would help you carry your bags in. Hazel will show you to your room. I'll go find her." He set Sophia's bags down next to the couch and headed out of the room to go find Hazel.

"Jonah?" Sophia said inquisitively, just seconds before he turned the corner and disappeared into the next room.

Jonah stopped and turned back around. "*Jah?*"

"It's a pleasure to meet you," Sophia said. She knew how word traveled quickly in a small town like Little Valley, and she desperately wanted to make a good first impression.

Jonah smiled back and nodded, briefly touching the brim of his hat. "I hope you enjoy your stay Ms. Adams."

After Jonah exited the room, Sophia turned to examine the handmade figurines on the shelves before turning to admire the beautiful quilt that hung on the wall next to the wood burning stove. In her career as a travel journalist for *Faith Afar* magazine, she had visited many wonderful Amish communities and seen so many beautiful, hand-crafted pieces. And she loved every minute of it. Sophia adored her job - it almost felt more like a beloved hobby. She was blessed to have been selected to travel and report back on all the different experiences she enjoyed so much.

"Welcome to the Amish Inn, Ms. Adams." A voice interrupted Sophia's thoughts.

"Ah, thank you! You must be Hazel?" Sophia turned around, brushing away a strand of strawberry blond hair that fell out of her messy bun and into her eyes.

"Yes, I am Hazel Thompson, the manager here. Come along and I'll show you the room we've prepared for you." It was clear to Sophia that Hazel was all business. She seemed to want to get right to the point so she could continue with whatever other tasks lay before her. She wore a fitted navy-blue suit dress with matching ballet flats, and Sophia couldn't imagine her wearing anything more casual. She was in mid-twenties, a petite woman, but her demeanor and her stiff posture seemed to give her some height and add a year or two to her age.

Sophia pulled up the handles of her suitcases and locked them in place so that she could roll them toward her room, one in each hand. She followed Hazel around the corner where Jonah had disappeared and into a long hallway. There were three closed doors on either side and a door, cracked open, at the very end. Hazel opened the second door on the right and entered the room ahead of Sophia. The room was small with just a bed, a nightstand and a dresser serving as furniture. Hazel walked to the windows and threw open the maroon-colored drapes, revealing beautiful sheer lace curtains. Sophia parked her suitcases just outside the closet door and approached the four-poster bed.

"This quilt is just beautiful," she said, tracing the lines of the stitching with her fingers.

"There is a luggage rack in the closet. The bathroom is down the hall. Lunch is not served here, but Heaven's Diner is right down the street, as well as a coffee shop. Dinner is served promptly at six o'clock. There is a weekly menu posted outside the kitchen in the dining area. Breakfast is served at eight o'clock each morning. So," Hazel looked at her watch before continuing, "the kitchen is currently closed." She listed all the information as if it were rehearsed a dozen times.

"Until six o'clock," Sophia said. "Got it." It was clear that Hazel lacked a bit of polished customer service, but she didn't mind. She couldn't wait to get out and explore the town.

Hazel nodded and turned to leave. "Enjoy your stay, Ms. Adams," she said over her shoulder as she shut the door behind her.

Sophia unpacked her clothes into the closet and dresser, selecting a clean comfortable outfit to change into for walking into town. She headed to the bathroom to freshen up. As she stepped out of her room, she instantly heard Hazel speaking in a tensed tone. As she walked past, Sophia determined that Hazel was having an intense phone conversation inside the second bedroom on the left, the door pulled closed but leaving a small crack. Not wanting to get caught eavesdropping, Sophia slipped inside the small bathroom and shut the door quietly. She placed her ear to the door, filled with curiosity.

"Look, I am NOT scared of you, so don't even try to threaten me. You have until tomorrow to move out of the house, or I'm calling the police." The sound of Hazel's footsteps drifted down the hallway as she exited the bedroom and turned back toward the living room.

Sophia grimaced at her reflection in the mirror. *No wonder she was so short with me,* she thought. Poor girl. There were few things worse than having to deal with a breakup, especially while you're at work. Sophia experienced something similar just recently herself, and she immediately felt a sense of compassion for Hazel.

After freshening up, Sophia returned to her room to grab her purse and her camera. She locked the door, chuckling to herself as she remembered what the driver had said, implying there was "danger" in Little Valley. She turned the corner into the living room and almost ran right into a middle-aged woman who was dusting the wood furniture. The small microfiber dust mop she was holding fell to the floor.

"Oh, pardon me," Sophia said sincerely. Both women bent to pick up the dust mop at the same time, but Sophia didn't grab it quick enough.

The woman looked at Sophia and then quickly looked away. In a low voice, she mumbled, "I'm so sorry, ma'am. I didn't see you there." Her eyes darted toward the dining area, and she fidgeted with her apron. Her name tag looked almost brand new, a stark contrast to the dark red polo shirt where it was pinned. The woman's name was Peggy.

"Oh, no. It was my fault," Sophia said. "I wasn't looking where I was going. It's nice to meet you, Peggy. My name is Sophia Adams."

Peggy tucked her straight hair behind her ear and with a much louder, more intentional voice, she said, "My pleasure. Can I help you find anything, Ms. Adams?" The words came out of her mouth methodically and sweet as sugar. She spoke loudly as if she hoped someone in the next room would hear that she was doing a good job, greeting the new guest. Her eyes again darted toward the dining area.

Sophia's eyes followed her glance and responded, "No, thank you. I think I'll just go check out the menu for tonight. I believe Hazel said it was posted in the dining room?"

Again, with a boisterous voice, Peggy answered, "Yes, the menu is right through there, tacked on the bulletin board on the left." She smiled what looked to Sophia like a forced smile and returned to dusting the furniture.

Sophia thanked Peggy for her help and walked toward the dining room. She found the menu exactly where she said it would be, on the left wall. As she was reading the list of breakfast and dinner items, she could again hear Hazel's voice. But this time, she was speaking to a gentleman in the kitchen next door, and she no longer sounded angry. Actually, it was quite the opposite.

"Hank, I really need a room for a couple of nights. You can take it out of my pay, if you want, but I have someth ing..." Hazel paused briefly, "...something personal going on." She wasn't able to hide the desperation in her words, if she was trying to do so.

Hank responded quickly with a kind voice, "Sure, Hazel, I don't have a problem with that. You can take an empty room for as long as you need to get things sorted."

"Thank you," Hazel responded, followed by what sounded to Sophia very much like a sigh of relief.

Sophia thought she heard their footsteps approaching and decided that she could only stand and look at the menu for so long before seeming suspicious. So she headed out the front door, passing Peggy again and wishing her a good day. Once on the porch, she took a deep breath of fresh air, headed down the porch steps, and turned left to- wards Main Street. She couldn't wait to find the Heaven's Diner that Hazel had mentioned earlier.

# Chapter Two

———◆———

Beth stood and stretched her arms toward the ceiling, arching her back. Her right cheek had flour smeared from where she had wiped her face with the back of her hand. Strands of hair had escaped from her *kapp* and framed her face. "Does anyone want a cup of coffee?" She was ready for a break from the baking and prep she had been doing since dawn with her twin sister, Anna, and their second cousin, Eva.

"*Jah*, I'm ready for a break," Anna responded. She slid off the stool she had been sitting on while kneading dough and wiped her hands on her apron. She stretched her arms high just as her twin sister had done a minute before, and Eva grinned as she watched.

"Sometimes it feels like I'm living in a world of *Deja vu* with the two of you," Eva said with a chuckle. "I'll start a fresh pot of coffee. You two relax."

The twins smiled at their younger cousin and laughed along with her. "*Jah*, we've heard that a few times over our lifetime," Beth said as she looked adoringly at her sister.

"I think we probably drive our husbands a little bit crazy sometimes," Anna chimed in.

Beth nodded, brushing the hair away from her forehead and tucking it back under her *kapp*. "It's true. Noah and Eli have put up with a lot over the years."

"Well, I love it," Eva interjected. "It's rather endearing." She collected the coffee mugs they had used earlier that morning from around the kitchen and began to wash them in the sink.

"*Denki*, Eva," Anna said. "Speaking of endearing, do we know when Rachel and Jacob will get to meet their baby yet? I haven't had a chance to catch up with you since you met up with Rachel yesterday, Beth. How is she?"

Beth twisted slowly right and left at the waist, her arms reaching out from her sides. "Oh, they are all so excited for the new baby, I'll tell ya. Their home is full of happiness and anticipation right now. You will have to go see how they've prepared for her when you have a chance. That extra bedroom in their home has been empty for so long, and now, there is a beautiful crib and a rocking chair, that Jacob built, of course."

Rachel and Jacob struggled to have children naturally for many years due to a medical condition. Their daughter, Grace, was born unexpectedly, surviving despite the odds, and the community knew that she was a gift from God for the couple. Even though Grace was a beautiful, wonderful surprise, Rachel and Jacob continued to pray for another chance to grow their family. They had been on a list for an adoption for many years, and now their dream was finally coming true.

Settling back down on the edge of her stool, Beth continued, "They meet with the adoption agency again early next week, but I think the baby is due anytime now. The mother has met the family, and they have all agreed to an open adoption, from what I understand."

Eva set a clean cloth filter into the funnel-shaped top of the pour over coffee maker. "Hm... What does an open adoption look like?" she asked as she added a few heaping teaspoons from the container of freshly ground coffee beans to the filter.

"Well, it can mean different things, really," Anna responded, and Beth nodded in agreement. "We've known a few families that have adopted children over the years, and more times than not, it is an open adoption of some sort."

"*Jah*, and it has always been successful," Beth interjected. "It's basically whatever the mother and the family agree upon, and with the Schwartz family, the agreement is that the mother will be allowed to stay in touch with a few visits each year. And Rachel and Jacob have also agreed to the mother taking photos of the baby, if she'd like. I know that was a tough decision for Jacob, but they trust that the mother will be respectful. And they understand how hard it can be to share such a precious gift."

"Ah, *gut*, I'm glad they were all able to come to a friendly agreement then," Eva said. "I can imagine that must be difficult sometimes. I wondered how an *Englischer* was going to feel about an Amish family raising her daughter."

"Where is the mother from, *Schwester*?" Anna asked Beth. "Surely she doesn't live in Little Valley?"

Beth shook her head. "She's from Stillson," she said. "But I don't know much more than that."

Eva tipped the tea kettle over the funnel, pouring hot water over the coffee grounds. "Well, the whole thing certainly sounds like a blessing," she said.

"Maybe we should plan a homecoming celebration for the Schwartz family, after they're feeling all settled," Anna said, shooting her twin sister a knowing smile.

"*Jah! Gut* idea!" Beth said, clapping her hands together and standing back on her feet. Planning parties was one of Beth's favorite things to do. She would take advantage of any excuse to celebrate, but this was definitely not just any excuse. This was a valid reason.

Eva filled the three mugs with the fresh aromatic hand-brewed coffee and dropped a couple sugar cubes in each. She placed a steaming hot cup in front of each of her cousins.

Anna took a small sip and complemented Eva on the coffee. "How are things coming along at the shop, dear?" Anna asked Eva.

Eva's shoulders slumped forward slightly. "Actually, I would love your advice on something," she said, rubbing the back of her neck.

Beth sat back down and both sisters set their eyes on Eva. "Of course, Eva, what is the matter?" Beth asked, worried. She had thought Eva was being more quiet than normal that morning, and at that moment, Eva looked uncomfortable.

"Well, there is this lady, Olivia Black. She owns the *Englisch* bakery in town, you know." Eva looked at each of the sisters.

The sisters nodded. They knew who Olivia Black was, and they had worried how things would be with Eva opening a new bakery. Especially since Sugar on Top had become an immediate success when it opened.

"Ms. Black comes in almost every afternoon and looks to see what is in my case. She always criticizes what I have on display, how it looks, or how it tastes. A lot of the time I will have other customers in the shop when she's saying these things. I just don't know how to deal with her. I don't want to ask her to leave or come across as mean in any way. I want to do the right thing, but I also want it to stop." Eva's words fell out of her mouth, her monotone voice growing more and more quiet. "Can you help?"

Beth walked over and draped her hand over Eva's shoulders, comforting her with a close hug. "I'm sorry this is happening, Eva," she said sincerely.

Anna nodded and reached out to place her hand on top of Eva's and said, "*Jah*, this is *baremlich*. We could talk to Olivia, but I don't think that is the right answer." Her eyes squinted and her brow furrowed as she thought about the advice she wanted to give.

Beth interjected. "First of all, Eva, you know that your desserts and pastries are truly delicious and wonderful. You have clearly already started making a name for yourself in town. Olivia wouldn't be doing this if that weren't true."

Eva nodded.

"I think the only thing you can do is communicate with Olivia and try to come to an agreement that is a win-win for both of you," Anna said.

Beth agreed and said, "Maybe there is something each of you sells that is a bit unique that you could each offer to your customers."

"Or maybe the two of you could enter the county fair's baking competition together," Anna said.

Eva perked up. "Oh, I do like those ideas! I will approach Olivia and see what she thinks. *Denki*, Anna and Beth!"

"Of course. Keep us posted on what you decide," Beth said with a warm smile. She loved it when she and her sister were in sync and could help someone work out a problem.

Anna stood and collected the empty coffee cups. She walked to the sink and began washing the dirty dishes piled next to the sink. "Well, let's clean up here. I think we have enough of what we need for this weekend's market sales."

Beth and Eva agreed and began to clean their work-stations. Beth asked, "How is everything else at the shop going, Eva?"

"Otherwise, things are going very well," Eva responded with a smile. "Business is really booming. There's a line every morning. I really don't know what I would do without Peggy's help."

"Is Peggy doing ok? Jonah tells me that she is such a hard worker at the inn, too. She certainly does have a busy schedule balancing both jobs," Beth said between sips.

"It's true," Eva nodded. "She has two school-aged daughters that she raises alone, and she doesn't make enough money at either job to pay all of her bills, I guess. She often seems on edge and it's not uncommon for her to be fighting tears when we're alone doing prep together in the early mornings. The other day, she became emotional talking about how grateful she is for her job at the bakery. I guess the manager at the inn is really not very nice to her."

"Ah, Jonah mentioned something similar the other day. Since Hank let Hazel start running things at the inn, I guess there are quite a few unhappy people working there. Jonah says she can be quite mean, and he did mention that Hazel and Peggy especially are at odds most of the time." Beth felt her heart tug for Peggy. She couldn't imagine the pressure that comes along with being a single mother, especially without a community like theirs to help.

"Well, hard work will bring reward. Peggy is doing the right thing, and Hazel may just be adjusting to her new responsibilities, as well. I'm sure things will smooth out before too long," Anna interjected.

Eva set her cup down and stood, adjusting her *kapp* and straightened her apron. "That's a *gut* point, Anna. I really like Peggy, and I hope she can find happiness."

"And time for rest, too. Hard work brings rewards, *jah*, but sometimes people can push themselves right over the edge, too. A lack of sleep can take its toll on your body both physically and emotionally. It's important that she takes care of herself," Beth said before taking her last sip. She made a mental note to add Peggy and her daughters to her daily prayers.

# Chapter Three

Dark clouds hovered in the sky above the color-ful covered booths that lined the outside edges of Tulip Park. The Little Valley Farmers' Market took place every week from Spring through Fall, rain or shine. Business owners of all types were busy setting up their booths with tents and awnings to keep their goods covered, as well as offer a dry retreat for their customers.

Beth had grown to love the energy that surrounded her and her sister every weekend as they manned their table of baked goods. She could still remember the first time she and Anna had set up shop in Tulip Park. She had been so nervous, her stomach in knots and her hands trembling as she collected the cash and packaged the cookies. She wasn't sure if her comfort level now was due to all the years of repetition or the effort she had put into learning to live with her condition. When Beth was diagnosed with high-functioning autism as a teenager, she was partially relieved to have an explanation for her discomfort in some social situations, her struggle with perfectionism, and her many obsessions. She could see how the way she acted and lived affected those closest to her, especially her twin sister, but she struggled daily with trying to be different to accommodate everyone else. Finally finding an explanation for her quirky ways brought understanding and acceptance for both her and her family members, and the twins grew closer as a result.

"What in the world are you thinking about over there?" Anna asked Beth, interrupting her thoughts. Anna was busy setting their table. She placed a silver tray of lemon bars lightly dusted with powdered sugar on the right side of the table and Beth reached over to adjust it slightly so that it lined up perfectly with the tray of fudge brownies sitting next to it in the center of the table.

"I was just remembering our first time out here, actually," Beth said with a small smile. She began placing her beautifully decorated sugar cookies on another tray. She was taking great care so as not to smudge the design on each. The sisters had spent a good amount of time designing each cookie, drawing either a hummingbird, a ladybug or a bumble bee on each. The sugar cookies were a fan favorite, and their most popular item each week. At some point, Anna had a wonderful idea to make smaller versions to offer as free cookies for all the children at the market. It was a brilliant thought because not only did the sisters get to see and visit with all the wonderful children, which they loved, but their sales increased as more and more little hands pulled their parents to the booth each week.

Anna chuckled, "*Ach du lieva*, you were so nervous, *Schwester*. I thought we'd never get through the day!"

Beth shrugged lightheartedly. "*Jah*, and look at me now," she said, a wide grin spread across her face as she stretched her arms out wide. "Well, that was a long time ago," Beth said, drawing out the word long dramatically, shifting her focus back to the setup.

Anna nudged Beth with her elbow and nodded her head as if to point inconspicuously. Beth followed Anna's gaze across the park. There she saw their friend, the *Englisch* diner owner, Jessica McLean, holding up one end of a booth tent. Matthew Beiler was bent over pounding the stake into the ground to secure the tent.

Matthew was the best friend of Anna's son-in-law, Moses, and he had become very much like part of their family since he had returned to the community. Years before, Matthew had decided not to return for baptism after his *Rumspringa,* but when a visit brought him back to Little Valley, he had a change of heart and decided that he indeed wanted to stay. He had not yet been baptized, but discussion and planning were in the works.

Anna and Beth - and several other people in the town - couldn't help but notice the chemistry that Matthew and Jessica shared. They had become fast friends and had been spending time together. Matthew ate lunch at Heaven's Diner nearly every day, and now Jessica was helping Matthew man his booth at the market. Since Matthew was living among the Amish community, it was assumed that he would date and marry an Amish woman, but there was no secret that he seemed to be fancying Jessica quite a bit instead.

"Have you asked Moses if he knows Matthew's intentions for Jessica?" Beth couldn't help but wonder if Jessica was why Matthew had not yet become baptized, and she prayed for each of them at night to help find their paths, whether it be together or apart.

"Oh goodness, no. It is not my place to pry into other people's business like that," Anna responded curtly.

Beth rolled her eyes and only had to wait a quick second before Anna continued, "I mean, I didn't ask Moses, but Sarah did confirm that Matthew is a bit conflicted about where he would stand with the community if Matthew were to pursue dating Jessica. She says that Matthew does want to rejoin the faith, but we can all see that he and Jessica have some sort of connection."

Beth smiled and nodded, "*Jah*, I believe a blind man could see that." She chuckled under her breath because of Anna's initial reaction to the question. She knew her sister well enough to know that Anna and her oldest daughter Sara, Moses' wife, had definitely discussed it.

"Sarah says that Matthew has an appointment with Bishop Packer soon. We can only assume he will be discussing his feelings, and maybe his future with Jessica then." After a brief pause, Anna quickly muttered, "You know I hate to gossip. I care very much for both Matthew and Jessica, and I want the best for both of them."

"Of course, *Schwester*. Since when do you worry that sharing things with your twin sister is considered gossip? Besides, I would've most likely have been part of the conversation with Sarah if I could've been there for dinner on Sunday myself," Beth assured her sister.

"*Jah*, that's true. I missed having you there. How did it go at Abigail's? Was Noah able to help Jeremiah finish setting up space in his barn for the leathersmithing business?" Anna rested back on her wooden folding chair. Their booth was all set up and ready for the farmers' market to begin, and now there were a few minutes to spare.

Beth welcomed the time to catch up with her sister, and she wanted to tell her all about how excited her daughter and son-in-law were about their new venture. "*Jah*, Jeremiah has everything he needs now. They are both really looking forward to Jeremiah working from home now. He has learned everything he can from the store and has started to build a clientele of his own. His hard work over the years has definitely paid off and his family will be able to reap the rewards now. Noah and I are so happy for them."

Abigail was Beth's oldest daughter. She had married Jeremiah several years before when they were both very young. Jeremiah did not have much ambition nor any real developed trades at that time, and because of this, Beth and Noah were not optimistic at first that Jeremiah would be able to successfully support their family. Beth and her husband shared a huge sense of relief that Jeremiah was beginning to prove them both wrong.

"That's such *gut* news," Anna said, smiling. "We will have to tell everyone about his new business, then."

"Business? Someone has a new business?" The sisters' conversation was interrupted by a deep husky voice. The two women looked up to find Sheriff Mark Streen standing in front of their booth. They rose to their feet, excited to see him.

"Where did you come from?" Anna asked, her face beaming. Beth and Anna had developed a close friendship with the sheriff when he had first come to town several months ago. The three of them, along with Deputy Chris Jones, had been given a nickname among the Little Valley town folk as the "Fearless Four Detective Squad" because they had put their heads together to solve a couple of pretty scary crimes that had put everyone on edge. Beth and Anna wore their imaginary badges with honor and were proud to say that they had helped put the criminals behind bars to protect their beautiful hometown.

"Well, I must be your first customer since I'm finding the two of you sitting down with nothing to do," Mark teased. "How are you ladies doing? I feel like I haven't seen you in a couple weeks."

"We're doing well," Beth answered. "Has it really been a couple of weeks already?"

"What about you, Sheriff? Enjoying the peace and quiet?" Anna asked, assembling a small care package for him.

"Oh, yes, it has been wonderful. Deputy Jones and I have gotten in a lot of fishing lately, which is a welcomed change. How is the community doing? I'm sure there have been wonderful barn raising parties since the fires that were set a few months ago. Are things feeling more settled again, I hope?"

Beth nodded, "Oh, *jah*. Things have returned to normal, and the community is thriving again."

"We're pretty resilient, it's true," Anna said, handing Mark the small box of goodies. "It's back to being boring again," Anna said, winking at her sister.

Mark laughed and said, "Well, let's see if we can keep it that way, ladies." He thanked the sisters for the package. "So, who has a new business? I know it's the devil's work to eavesdrop, but I couldn't help but overhear you two talking about it when I walked up."

"Beth's son-in-law, Jeremiah Baker," Anna answered.

"*Jah*, my husband just helped him set up shop in his barn. He is a very talented leather smith." Beth's face beamed with pride.

"Good for him! I will pass the word around." Then Mark changed the subject as if he just remembered something, "Have you met the new reporter yet?"

Beth and Anna glanced at each other briefly before Anna responded, "No, not yet. Have you met her?"

"No, but I did run into Hank last night at the store, and he said she had arrived; you know, she's staying at the inn there. I was wondering how long it would be before she tracked down the two notorious twins for an interview." He grinned.

"Well, we're pretty easy to find, so..." Beth's voice trailed off, and she hoped it wasn't too obvious that something about that meeting felt a little ominous to her.

"True, true," said Mark. "Well, you let me know if things get out of hand. I'm sure everything will be fine, but just in case. You know where to find me."

Anna pressed her lips together in a close-lipped smile. "We'll be just fine, Sheriff. We've faced a lot worse than a simple interview with a reporter from a nationally recognized faith tourism magazine."

Beth reached out and grabbed Anna's hand hidden by the height of the table and squeezed it. Maybe it was a "post-traumatic stress" sort of thing, but Beth felt a familiar sense of dread sitting like a heavy anchor right in the middle of her stomach.

# Chapter Four

The bell hanging from the door handle chimed as it knocked against the glass, announcing the arrival of another guest.

"Welcome to Heaven's Diner, please grab a seat anywhere you'd like," Jessica called out from behind the counter. An attractive woman in her mid-thirties with shoulder-length blonde hair approached the counter directly across from Jessica, pulled out a high seat and settled in. She removed her cross-body purse and then the heavy camera from around her neck, placing them both on the counter.

"Hi, I'm Sophia Adams. This is your diner, I presume?" She asked with a voice both friendly and professional.

Jessica eyed the camera and tried to hide her suspicion. It's not like Jessica had never had tourists in her diner before, but she had become more wary and less trusting of them lately as the number of strangers grew. More and more, Little Valley was falling victim to prejudice and a general lack of respect for the Amish community that lived in town, and Jessica had zero tolerance for any of that. She had established close friendly relationships with several members of their community, and she would not stand for any harm to come their way.

"Yes, I'm the owner. Name's Jessica McLean. Where are you from?" Jessica spoke with a Southern accent as thick as molasses that could be mistaken for friendly despite the tone.

"Nice to meet you, Jessica. I'm here from Chicago. I'm a journalist with the *Faith Afar* magazine. Our main office is out there. I'll tell you what, Little Valley sure is a beautiful town. It's nice to get away from the city." Sophia brushed her bangs out of her eyes.

Jessica was intrigued and she was starting to let her guard down. "Oh wow, I don't know that I've ever met anyone from Chicago. What kind of magazine is *Faith Afar*? I've never heard of it." She passed a laminated menu over to her guest.

Sophia was used to this question. Although it was considered a national magazine, it was still small beans compared to something like *National Geographic* or *Time Magazine.* "It's a magazine about faith tourism. Have you ever heard of faith tourism?" Sophia asked.

Jessica shook her head, but she suspected she knew why Sophia was in Little Valley.

"Well, faith tourism can mean different things to different people. Some people travel on sort of pilgrimages, you know for religious or spiritual purposes, and some people consider faith tourism as more of a way to learn more about different cultures and religions, kind of like sightseeing different religious monuments and communities. *Faith Afar* is more about the sightseeing part of faith tourism."

"So, let me guess. You're here to document the Amish community in Little Valley," Jessica said, with her hands on her hips.

"Yes, that's right," Sophia said calmly and with a matter-of-fact tone.

"Well, I'll cue you in right away then, that the Amish community doesn't like their photo taken." She nodded toward the large professional camera sitting on the counter next to Sophia's purse.

Sophia responded quickly, "Oh, yes, I know. I have no intention of disrespecting their wishes. I will only be taking photos of scenery... and maybe a horse or two, if I'm lucky." She smiled warmly.

Jessica's shoulders relaxed slightly, and she let out a slow breath. "Oh, ok. They're really good people, you know, and they've been through a lot lately. I just don't want anything else bad to happen to anyone. I hope you understand."

Sophia raised her left eyebrow and said, "Oh, yes, no harm whatsoever. I completely understand your concerns. Thank you for letting me know. So, can you tell me what has happened..."

Sophia's sentence was cut off by raised voices from the corner back booth.

Jessica mumbled under her breath, "I'll be right back to take your order." She headed toward the direction of the noise. "Is everything ok over here?" She called out as she approached, order pad in hand. She ripped off the piece of paper she had prepared earlier with their order total and set it down on the table. She hoped that would be a sign to wrap things up and head out if the couple was going to have an argument.

"We're fine," the girl said through gritted teeth, glaring at the young man sitting across from her.

"Hazel will pay the ticket today," the man said. "She always has extra cash in her pocket," he said loudly as if he wanted to let everyone in on the conversation. Jessica thought, *I wonder if I should tell him there isn't really much of an audience here,* but she knew that wasn't helpful, just snarky.

Hazel looked as if steam could shoot out of her ears at any point. Her face was bright red, and her hands were on the table in front of her, her fists clenched, her knuckles white. Jessica worried that she might start swinging at the young man sitting across from her. He sat with an expression that looked as if he were enjoying Hazel's fury. He pushed the ticket her way, grabbed his cell phone and stuck it in his pocket, and said in a calm voice, "If you think I'm moving out, you're delusional. I'm on the lease, too. If you wanted to move out and live in that stupid Amish Inn for the rest of your life, I would encourage you to do so." As he stood, he leaned in closer and said one final thing that sent chills down Jessica's spine, "Karma's comin' for you, Hazel." He winked and clicked his teeth and then turned and walked out of the diner.

"Are you ok, honey?" Jessica asked, gently touching Hazel's shoulder. She could see the young lady's eyes welling up with tears, and she immediately felt bad for her. "You know what, don't you even worry about this check," Jessica said, collecting the ticket off the table and slipping it back into her apron. "This one is on the house."

Hazel glanced up at Jessica and without a word, she scrambled to collect her cell phone and purse and hurried towards the door. She stopped dead in her tracks when she saw Sophia sitting at the counter. Her face turned a deeper red, she immediately turned away and dropped her face toward the floor before picking up the pace and exiting the diner.

Jessica quickly returned to the counter and apologized to Sophia for the scene. "I swear, I shoulda named this place Drama Diner! But you know, Heaven's Diner just sounds so much more welcoming, doesn't it?" She chuckled, trying to make light of the situation.

Sophia laughed, "Well, there's all kinds of people in this world, for sure. I didn't even see them over there. I thought I was the only customer."

"Life is full of surprises, I guess," Jessica said. Then wanting to change the subject, she asked, "So, what do you feel like? Have you had a chance to look at the menu yet?"

"Oh, I don't even need to see a menu to know that I want to try one of those cinnamon rolls in your case there,"

Sophia said, pointing towards the glass bakery case, "unless you think there's a better choice in there."

"Oh yes, you can't go wrong with the cinnamon rolls. They're my favorite. Made right here in town, of course, by my good friends, Anna and Beth." She grabbed a clean plate and reached in with a spatula to grab the last cinnamon roll out of the case. "Anna and Beth have a booth down at the Farmers' Market every week and their baked goods are really just all so good. Now, you can get delicious baked goods like theirs at a new bakery in town called Sugar on Top. It's actually owned by Anna and Beth's cousin, Eva Zook. She learned everything she knows from those two wonderful, and very talented, women."

Just a moment after she had finished her last sentence and set the plate in front of Sophia, the bell on the door chimed again.

"Well, it's like I mentioned your name and you appeared!" Jessica squealed and ran around the counter to greet her dear friends. "It's so good to see y'all!" She hugged the twin sisters and when she saw the box Anna was holding in her hand, she exclaimed "Ooooh, tell me you brought me more goodies!"

"*Jah*, but this time we brought you some of Eva's new cream horns. You'll have to try them. They've become so popular at the bakery." Anna said with a wide smile.

Jessica noticed Beth was looking at Sophia sitting at the counter, and knowing Beth, she was sure that she had already spied the camera on the counter next to her. "Come on in and meet Sophia, Anna and Beth," Jessica said, recognizing the opportunity to help set the tone for their first encounter with the journalist.

Sophia rose to her feet and bowed her head slightly in the twins' direction. Anna and Beth exchanged quick glances with raised eyebrows. "Hi, I'm Sophia Adams," she said.

"*Hallo*, I'm Anna Miller and this is Beth Troyer." Anna said stiffly. Beth remained silent.

Noticing a bit of nervous tension, Jessica asked the sisters, "Won't you stay for a cup of coffee and a snack, Anna and Beth?"

Anna looked at Beth and Beth silently nodded approval to Anna. Anna spoke, "Sure, Jessica. We'll stay for a bit."

Jessica clasped her hands together, "Oh, good! Would you like to grab a seat at the counter this time? Or do you prefer a booth?"

Beth spoke for the first time, "We'll sit at the counter," she said and the two women sat on the left side of Sophia, Anna in the middle.

Once everyone was settled, Jessica set coffee mugs in front of all three women and placed one for herself on the opposite side of the counter. She poured steaming fresh coffee into each and offered sugar packets and creamer.

"So, Anna and Beth, Sophia is a journalist with a faith tourism magazine," Jessica said, breaking the awkward silence.

Anna and Beth remained looking forward towards Jessica, sipping their coffee in unison.

"Yes, that's right," Sophia interjected. "I'm here to learn, and write about, your wonderful community. I've traveled a bit to different Amish communities across the country, and I have nothing but respect for your faith and beliefs. I am always fascinated to meet new people and find similarities and differences from community to community, not just with the Amish but with the *Englischers* who live among them, as well."

Beth and Anna remained silent.

"I would love to spend some time with you, when it is convenient for you, of course. And only if you are comfortable with that." Sophia looked at her camera and then quickly said, "Oh, and I have no intention of taking photos of anything that you would find offensive. You should know that."

Anna turned to look at Sophia, and Beth followed suit. "Thank you. My sister and I could find some time to spend with you to help you write your story. We have a wonderful community here in Little Valley. We were actually expecting you, so it's good to meet you here in person."

Beth nodded and agreed, "We could show you around, if you'd like."

Sophia's face beamed, "Wonderful! That makes me so happy! Where shall we meet? When would you be free?"

Beth responded, "Why don't you come by tomorrow for lunch, if that works well for you?" Anna nodded.

"Perfect!" Sophia responded, excitement in her voice.

Jessica smiled. "Now, this is what Heaven's Diner is all about. Flourishing friendships, both new and old."

"Talk about being in the right place at the right time! I had the chance to try this cinnamon roll - oh my gosh, it's so good! And then I got to meet all of you wonderful women!

"Heaven's Diner is the perfect name for this place, Jessica," Sophia said with a wink and a grin.

# Chapter Five

———⬥———

After tightening the last screw on the door hinge to the "yellow room," Jonah bent over and placed the screwdriver back in the toolbox neatly, lining it up with the others before closing the lid and latching it shut. He stood and slowly opened and closed the door a few times to make sure his repair was sufficient. The door was no longer sticking, so he was satisfied.

After closing and locking the door, Jonah headed toward the kitchen. He knew that there was a staff meeting scheduled, and he wanted to be early to continue to set a good impression. He was enjoying his job as the inn's handyman, and he hoped that Hank Davis, the owner, was happy with his work.

When he entered the room, he was surprised to see the new chef, Emily, already there. She was brewing coffee and had set out cookies for the meeting. "Hi, Jonah," she greeted him warmly.

"Hi, Emily," Jonah said, removing his hat and holding it in his right hand by his side. "How are you today?"

Emily smiled, "I'm fantastic. How are you?"

"Very well, indeed. How are you getting along with your new job?" Jonah asked, as he reached for a cookie. With one bite, he thought they didn't compare to his mother and aunt's famous sugar cookies, but he would never tell Emily that in risk of hurting her feelings.

"Everything is going good, thank you. I'm starting to get comfortable with the kitchen, getting to know where everything is, and keeping up with the schedule of meals and all." Emily said, reaching for a cookie herself and sitting down on one of the chairs brought in from the dining area for the meeting.

"I have heard the guests compliment your food," Jonah said, honestly. "I think you're doing a nice job."

"Thank you," Emily said, bringing her hand to her heart. "That is really nice to hear. I like it here."

Hank walked in and joined the conversation. "We like havin' you here, Emily," he said.  His voice was often boisterous, as if he were commanding the room's attention. At first, his tone had made Jonah nervous, but now Jonah was growing accustomed to it.

Emily smiled at Hank and said, "It's so good to be here. I really appreciate the opportunity."

Hank nodded and turned his attention to Jonah, "Hey, there, Jonah. How's it goin'?  You got enough work to keep you busy around here?" The sarcasm wasn't lost on Jonah.

"Oh, yes, plenty to do," said Jonah, grinning. "I like to keep busy, though."

Sebastian entered the room, "What? Who's not busy?" He joked. His Southern accent weighed down his words to where almost everything he said sounded like he was slurring. He slapped Hank on the back. "How's it goin' ol' man?"

"Sebastian!" Hank said loudly and extended his hand. The two men clasped hands and pulled each other in for a casual half hug. Jonah watched and felt a tinge uncomfortable. He wished he had a close relationship like that with his boss, Hank, but he also wasn't very good at physical connection, even a masculine half hug, with anyone outside of his family.

"Well, I'm on time. Where's the other girls?" Sebastian said, shoving a cookie in his mouth.

"I'm here," Hazel said as she walked into the room. "I would've been here earlier if I hadn't had to beg the city permit inspector to overlook your pile of weeds as a fire hazard in our meeting just now."

"What are you even talkin' about?" Sebastian snapped at Hazel. "You're makin' stuff up."

"I'm not," Hazel responded, her shoulders back, and a clipboard held tight to her chest. "A *real* gardener would know not to put a pile of dead weeds and dry brush so close to the building." She looked over at Hank and rolled her eyes.

"I was gonna move it, Hank," Sebastian said, sounding almost like a child wanting his father to choose a side between an argument with his sister. "I swear I just put it there, and I was gonna move it this afternoon. I didn't even know that we had an inspector coming." He glared at Hazel.

Hazel ignored Sebastian and looked at Hank with a blank stare. Hank spoke up and said, "Ok, ok, Sebastian, just make sure you clean it up today. Thank you, Hazel, for lettin' us know."

Hazel shook her head slowly, clearly frustrated and changed the subject. "Where is Peggy? She is the whole reason we have to meet in the afternoon like this. Don't tell me she's not going to show."

Hank responded, "I'm sure she'll be here soon. We still got three minutes until it's four o'clock."

Hazel rolled her eyes and let out a loud sigh.

"Would you like a cookie, Hazel?" Emily asked sincerely.

Hazel snapped, "No." Then, in a mocking tone, she said, "I don't want a cookie, Emily." Turning to look at Hank, she said, "If she's not here by four, I think we need to take some kind of disciplinary action. I'm so tired of everybody having to work around her schedule all the time."

Peggy walked in, with her head held low, and without a word, she sat next to Jonah.

Hank spoke up, "Here she is! Hi, Peggy! You made it!"

Peggy raised her face and said, "Yes, I'm sorry I wasn't here sooner. I came as soon as I could." She looked over at Hazel who was furiously writing something on her clipboard.

"No worries, Peggy. You weren't late." Hank reassured her. "Now, let's get started," Hank said, motioning for Hazel to begin the meeting. Sebastian took the seat on the other side of Peggy and Emily sat next to him. Their chairs formed a semi-circle facing Hank and Hazel.

Hazel pulled up a high stool and took her time getting settled. She held her clipboard in her hand and scanned a few pieces of paper behind the one on top. Then, after another moment, Hazel cleared her throat and began. "Well, now that we're all here," she started, looking directly at Peggy, "we can get right to business.

"Let's start with you, Emily. We want to check in with you and see how you are getting settled. I will say that the dinners have been on time, but I personally think they could be a little bit tastier. The stew you made the other night really lacked seasoning. What did you think, Hank?" Hazel turned to look at Hank.

Emily shifted in her seat.

"I actually thought it was very good. I thought it tasted authentic to an Amish dinner, but what did you think, Jonah?" Hank asked.

Jonah felt his cheeks turn pink. "I didn't eat any of the meal, sir. My shift ends before the dinner hour, but I am happy to try anything and give you my opinion if you ever want it." He paused briefly before continuing, "I did hear a customer say they really thought dinner was delicious the night before. I'm not sure what meal it was, but I have heard compliments. I was telling Emily that earlier."

Hazel shifted her glaring eyes to Jonah, but before she could speak, Hank interjected, "Well, that's a good thing.

Thank you, Jonah." Then, turning to Emily, he said, "Emily, if you ever wanna test the authenticity of your food, please don't hesitate to ask Jonah for his opinion."

Emily nodded and smiled gratefully at Jonah.

Hazel interrupted, "Ok," she said, sounding more annoyed than when the meeting first started. "Moving on." She looked right at Sebastian, and he sat up taller in his seat. "Sebastian." Hazel hesitated after pronouncing his name. "Do you happen to know when you will finally get to pruning the flower beds in front of the inn? It's actually starting to look unkempt. It's honestly embarrassing."

Sebastian answered quickly, "I started that today. It's a big renovation project, really, but I am hoping to make some headway on it before the end of the week."

Hank jumped in again, recognized Sebastian's hard work and assured him that he trusted his abilities. He turned to Hazel and said, "What's next?"

It was Hazel's turn to look a little bit flushed, and she fumbled again with the paper on her clipboard. "Jonah, do you have any updates for us today?" There was a hint of defeat in her voice when she asked the question.

Jonah pulled out a small notebook from his chest pocket, reviewed his completed projects with the group and listed the ones that remained to be tackled. Hank again seemed pleased and complimented Jonah on his hard work. "I don't know what we would do without you here, Jonah," he said. Jonah let out a small sigh of relief and thanked Hank for the recognition.

"Well, I guess that leaves Peggy," Hazel said, emphasizing Peggy's name as if it were something she disliked. Jonah looked over at Peggy and watched her straighten her back and lift her face to Hazel's, meeting her stare. There was an awkward silence; a thick fog of tension hung in the air. Jonah wasn't sure why these two were always at odds, but he had witnessed a few times where Hazel treated Peggy pretty poorly. In addition to chastising words, Jonah watched Hazel walk on Peggy's freshly mopped floors and then scold her for not doing a good job just one week prior. Another time more recently, Jonah saw Hazel dump a bag of trash on the floor and tell Peggy to clean it up immediately.

Jonah had been conflicted about what to do, and he carried a sense of guilt about not speaking up and defending Peggy or informing Hank. He had spoken to his father, Noah, about it recently, and Noah had suggested he pray and ask *Gotte* for a change of heart within Hazel and for strength within Peggy. Jonah had taken his father's advice and had been including Hazel and Peggy in his daily prayers. At that moment, watching Peggy prepare for her face-off with Hazel in front of the group, he closed his eyes and prayed silently one more time.

"As you all probably know, I stayed in the yellow room last night," Hazel said, maintaining eye contact with Peggy, "and am I glad I did. Because I got to see firsthand what our customers are seeing." The group nodded. Jonah opened his eyes. "Well, it's not great. I'm going to tell you. The door was sticking, which Jonah fixed, thank you, Jonah. And the room was filthy. I don't know when the last time the floors were mopped or the rug vacuumed. The bed was very sloppily made, and there was a layer of dust on the nightstand and on top of the picture frames." Hazel paused, and Peggy held fast with locking eyes and conserving her emotionless face. "Do you want to explain yourself, Peggy? I mean, what do you even do here?" Hazel raised her eyebrows and cocked her head as she sent the question directly to the woman across from her.

Peggy looked at Hank, and Hank nodded. His eyes were kind, unlike the cold eyes of the woman sitting next to him. Peggy took a deep breath and responded, "I can only imagine that you must be exaggerating, Hazel. I cleaned that room thoroughly just before you moved in there. I mopped the floors. I vacuumed the rug. I made the bed with clean sheets and professionally tucked the sheets and tightened the quilt on top, removing wrinkles. There isn't one bit of dust in this entire inn, because I take care of that daily. Everyone here has seen me dusting and cleaning. I stay busy, and I take pride in how I keep this place just as clean as I keep my own home." Jonah noticed that Peggy's voice was confident and steady.

Hazel began to argue, "Are you saying I'm..."

Hank reached out and stopped Hazel in mid-sentence by gently touching her forearm. "Thank you, Peggy. I have seen the work you do and I'm happy with the results. Hazel, I will come take a look at your room right after this meeting, and you can show me what you just described."

Hazel squirmed in her seat and pulled her arm out of Hank's reach. "This is such a waste of time," she muttered. "Hank, if everyone is doing such a great job, I guess we can all just go about our business as usual, then, and watch the decline of the Amish Inn. I'm done with this meeting." She stormed off, clipboard in hand. The team sat in silence, listening to her footsteps stomping away and the front door slamming shut.

The fog of tension that hung in the air moments before seemed to dissipate. Hank stood and spoke, "Well, I want to address the elephant in the room before we all get back to work. Hazel is going through some difficult times in her personal life, so I appreciate your patience with all of that. Let's just stay focused on the things we need to get done, create a welcoming atmosphere and provide a great service to our customers. Come to me if you have any questions for now."

The staff meeting was adjourned. Jonah agreed to help Sebastian clean up the pile of weeds before heading home, and Emily began to chop vegetables for dinner.

Before heading outside, Jonah watched Peggy approach Hank, wringing her hands, and asked, "Can I speak to you in private, Hank?"

"Of course, Peggy," Hank said, and the two headed towards Hank's office situated in the very back of the inn.

# Chapter Six

Sugar on Top had only been open an hour, but a line had formed all the way out the door. Eva and Peggy were busy greeting customers, packing desserts into small light pink to-go boxes or sliding pastries into small paper bags of the same color. The pinging sounds from the cash register and the small twinkling bells on the door almost created a catchy tune as they sounded out sometimes in unison, and sometimes simultaneously, barely heard over the humming of the crowd that stood patiently waiting their turn in line.

"Can I help who's next, please?" Eva called out after saying goodbye to a customer.

"Yes, good morning, Ms. Zook," a familiar voice spoke up. Eva recognized Sebastian right away. He was one of her most regular customers, purchasing the same butterscotch cream horn every single morning.

"Hi, Sebastian!" Eva said, wearing a big smile. "The usual today, I guess?" She asked as she made her way to the end of the case where only a few cream horns remained. The light and fluffy pastry filled with different flavors of cream and lightly dusted with powdered sugar was the bakery's most popular item.

"Yes, ma'am. You know I love those things," Sebastian said, grinning.

"Well, you're lucky you got in line when you did because it looks like this is the last of the butterscotch," Eva said, "although, I would be tempted to run back and throw a new batch in the oven for you since you have to be one of my very favorite customers."

Sebastian blushed, "Well, I would be pretty disappointed, but I wouldn't make you do that. I would just have to pick something else, I guess." He laughed.

"I know what I'll do. I'll just start saving one for you every day," Eva offered.

"That would be very gracious of you, ma'am. Thank you so much!" Sebastian's face beamed.

"It's no problem!" Eva slid the cream horn into a small pink paper bag, folded down the top and stuck a small sticker on it that read *Sugar on Top*. She had just received the new stickers in the mail, and she was thrilled with how they looked. The design on the sticker matched the design on her sign out front, a pink swirl created the capital letter *T* in the word top.

She handed Sebastian the paper bag and collected his money. "See you tomorrow," Eva said, "Thank you for stopping by today, Sebastian."

"Yep, see you tomorrow," Sebastian confirmed with a nod of the head. "Bye, Ms. Zook. Bye, Peggy, see you at work later on," he said as Peggy was filling a box of sugar cookies and danishes.

Peggy lifted her head and smiled back, "Yes, see you then, Sebastian! Have a good morning!" She closed the box and invited the customer to join her at the cash register.

Eva stood near the cash register, reaching below the counter for a bundle of paper bags to restock their supply.

Peggy muttered, "I just love that guy. He's so nice."

"Who? Sebastian?" Eva asked. Peggy seemed to be in a much better mood today, she noticed.

"Yes. Sebastian. He's the gardener at the inn, you know," she said before collecting her customer's cash and wishing her a nice day.

"Oh, I do think my cousin Jonah did say that, now that you mention it," Eva said. "He seems like a really nice guy. He has been coming in here every single morning, and he always orders the same thing. A butterscotch cream horn. So, I told him I would start saving one for him. Just so you know and can help me remember."

"Ah, that's very nice of you. I'm sure he'd love that. I'll help remember," Peggy said, drying her hands before pulling on a new set of disposable nitrile gloves.

The two women worked tirelessly to help all the customers waiting in line, and when things had quieted down, they turned their attention to the task of reorganizing the display case. They worked together efficiently pulling the empty trays out of the cases and consolidating what goodies were left, moving them to the front and center of the case.

"I'll tell you what, those cream horns are a hit," Peggy said, wiping a pan dry after washing it. "Do you think we're making enough of those? We always run out and have to tell the customers that they're gone."

Eva continued to collect the dirty pans and trays and set them next to the sink. She stepped in to wash, handing the cleaned dishes to Peggy to be dried. "I was actually thinking that same thing earlier. We are definitely going to have to reassess and make more cream horns in the mornings. We don't want our customers to go looking for them somewhere else."

"I don't know where they would even find anything like your cream horns," Peggy said with a grin.

Their conversation was interrupted by a high, squeaky voice, "Well, they could get cream puffs at my place."

Eva's stomach churned. She slowly turned around and found Olivia Black standing on the other side of the case. "Hi, Ms. Black," Eva said, hoping her voice exuded confidence even though she didn't feel it herself. "I was hoping I'd see you soon. I've been thinking about something, and I wanted to run it by you."

Olivia tilted her head to look over her glasses across the counter at Eva. Eva felt as if Olivia's eyes might pierce holes right through her own and she clasped her hands together in front of her, bracing herself against the trembles she felt.

"Um, so, I was thinking that maybe we could, um, think of some way that we could work, um, together," Eva stumbled through the words, and she hated how her own voice sounded so weak and scared.

Olivia continued to stare at Eva without a response. Her expression remained cold and unfriendly.

Eva knew she had to continue. "I mean, I don't know what that looks like, but my aunts were suggesting that maybe we could collaborate on something that would benefit both of us."

Olivia's eyes squinted further, and Eva wasn't sure exactly what that meant. So, she continued, "You know, since we are the only two bakeries in Little Valley."

Olivia finally spoke. "Oooh, so your aunts thought that we could work together, did they?" She asked, the words escaping her thin lips in a way that wasn't meant to be nice.

Eva suppressed a gasp. She had hoped that Olivia would warm up to her, but that wasn't happening.

"Listen here, Ms. Zook. I have no intention of helping you make any more money. I've been here much longer than you have - maybe even before you were born. Do you think I had someone helping me at the beginning with some sort of collaboration?" Olivia raised her hands in the air, moving the first two fingers on each of her hands, mimicking putting quotations on the word collaboration as if it were nonsensical.

"That's just ridiculous, and it's not..." Olivia continued, but she was abruptly interrupted.

"Then why do you come in here all the time?" Peggy snapped.

Eva was startled. She had never heard Peggy speak like that, and she wasn't sure how to react.

Olivia shifted her beady eyes toward Peggy, like an eagle who had spotted its next prey. "I beg your pardon. I can come and go wherever I please." She waited for a response.

Peggy stood tall and pushed her hair back out of her face. "I didn't say you couldn't come in here. I'm just curious why you need to come in here all the time if your business is doing so well."

Olivia looked back at Eva and said, "Am I able to purchase one of your cream horns, or is that too much to ask?"

Eva forced a smile and said, "Well, I wish I could sell one to you, Ms. Black, but unfortunately, we are all sold out. We only have the desserts that are left in the case for today."

Olivia scoffed, "Fine. What a waste of time this has been." She turned on her heel and headed out the door.

"Have a good day!" Eva and Peggy called out in unison and laughed as the door swung shut behind her.

"I'm sorry, Eva, I couldn't just stand there and let her be rude to you," Peggy said, touching Eva's arm.

"Thank you for stepping in, Peggy. I know it's not funny, but that woman is too much. She had me wound up like a top! And I was sincerely trying to find a way for us to become friendly." Eva collapsed in the chair by the small desk on the side of the kitchen.

"You don't deserve that. And I honestly don't know if Olivia has it in her to be friendly. I think she may be right - it may have just been a waste of time." Peggy said, her eyes kind and sympathetic. "Don't worry, though. Sugar on Top is really doing so well, and it's because your baking is so good. And people like you. Those are just two things that you have that she doesn't."

"I don't know. I've never been to Something Sweet. She must have something special to have stayed in business all these years." All of a sudden, Eva smacked herself in the forehead. "I forgot to mention the county fair's baking competition! I was going to ask her if she wanted to think about submitting something together to represent Little Valley."

Peggy rolled her eyes and grabbed the towel off the counter, letting it hang by her side. "Oh, Eva. You are quite the optimist." She shook her head and headed out to the tables at the front of the shop to wipe them down. "Some people just aren't good people. Unfortunately, I happen to know a few of them myself. And I take comfort in the fact that a person's intentions in life lead to either their success or their demise."

# Chapter Seven

---

Rays of sun streamed through the sheer lace curtains, gently waking Sophia as it touched her closed eyelids. She laid there for a few minutes, thinking about her time so far in the town of Little Valley. She enjoyed the time she had spent window shopping and especially meeting Jessica and the twins, Anna and Beth, in Heaven's Diner. She was looking forward to getting to know the sisters better later that afternoon.

She pushed herself up in bed and reached high, enjoying the stretch down her back. Standing on her feet, she winced. I will definitely be wearing my tennis shoes today, she thought to herself, glancing over at the ballet flats that were tossed in front of her closet from the day before when she explored the shops downtown.

Sophia drew back the curtains and could see the groundskeeper already at work, pulling weeds out of what looked like a container garden that was once beautiful but now needed much love and attention. He was kneeling, his back curved as he worked diligently creating a small pile of weeds next to him that grew larger with each addition.

"*Hallo*, Sebastian!" Sophia heard Jonah call out. She looked over and saw him, hand raised up in a wave. Sebastian turned and waved back, returning the friendly morning greeting. She watched as Jonah approached the garden and joined Sebastian in the same mirrored position. She could hear their cheerful voices, but she couldn't make out what they were saying. Instinctively, she reached for her camera, but before she raised it to her eye, she remembered her promise not to take photos of the Amish. She grabbed her notebook instead and wrote a few sentences describing the scene. Jonah looked exactly the same as when he first greeted her at the Amish Inn's front door. He was wearing the same black pants and white cotton shirt, almost as if it were a uniform. His hat sat perfectly positioned on his head, curly hair peeking out below the brim. His shoes were simple... and plain. *Plain is the perfect word to describe the Amish attire*, Sophia wrote. *Their plain clothing hints at a life of simplicity that makes city folk like myself a bit envious.*

She closed the notebook and threw on a pair of jeans and an emerald, green blouse that had embroidered flowers stitched around the hem. Grabbing her toiletry bag, she headed for the bathroom down the hall. She noticed that the room Hazel had been staying in the past two nights was left open a crack, but she kept her eyes straight ahead as she passed, allowing for the courtesy of privacy. She entered the bathroom, shut the door and performed her morning skincare regimen. She brushed her teeth and hair next, pinning up one side away from her face. She swept on a small amount of blush and mascara and headed back to her room to finish getting ready for the day. She was excited to visit the Coffee World. She had heard it was owned by an Amish gentleman, and she was especially looking forward to enjoying a hot chai tea latte.

Just as she passed Hazel's door, still cracked open, an alarm sounded. Sophia recognized the alarm tone as the same one she used when she had an appointment in the mornings. It was programmed in her cell phone. The timing of the alarm startled Sophia, and she jumped. But she managed to continue down the hallway, again without peering into Hazel's room. She put her toiletry bag back in the closet and grabbed her tennis shoes, sitting down to slip them on and lace them. She grabbed her camera again and her purse, and exited the room, closing the door behind her.

She paused outside of her door as the alarm continued to sound. A sense of worry overcame her as she realized that Hazel had not turned off the alarm yet, and it was definitely loud enough to wake someone. I hope everything is ok, Sophia thought, as she hesitated for another few seconds. She hoped the alarm would be turned off, and that Hazel was just a really heavy sleeper. But no such luck. The alarm continued to blare its repetitive loud buzzing noises. Sophia took a deep breath and decided it would be the right thing to check on Hazel. She approached the door which remained cracked open and peered inside. Hazel was lying on the bed on top of the sheets, her feet draped over the side. She looked as if she had been sitting on the edge of the bed, leaned over to lie back and fell fast asleep.

"Hazel?" Sophia said, quietly from the doorway. There was no answer. Hazel remained still.

Sophia knocked loudly on the door. The alarm continued to scream buzzing noises. The noise was definitely coming from a cell phone sitting on the bedside table next to an open pastry box. She called out Hazel's name again, a bit louder this time. When Hazel didn't respond, a chill ran down Sophia's spine and the hair on the back of her neck stood on end.

Sophia slowly approached the bed and reached out to gently nudge Hazel. She gasped. Hazel wasn't responding. There was definitely something wrong. Sophia ran out of the room to get help. As she turned the corner, she ran right into Hank.

"Whoa, Ms. Adams, everything ok? You look like you've seen a ghost." Hank said, holding onto her arms firmly as if to help keep her standing. Sophia was so grateful to find Hank so quickly. She had met him the day before and she instantly liked and trusted him after his warm welcome.

Sophia stuttered, "It's, it's Hazel. I'm afraid something's wrong with Hazel."

Hank's brow creased with worry, and he released his grip on Sophia as she gathered her posture. "I was just coming to check on the buzzing sound..." He passed by Sophia and headed down the hallway. Sophia followed him, explaining how she had noticed Hazel's door was cracked and then how she had found Hazel on her bed, unresponsive.

Hank pushed the door all the way open and called out to Hazel in a loud voice. He approached the side of the bed and grabbed her wrist, checking for a pulse. "Oh, no," he said quietly, shaking his head. "Oh, no. This can't be happening."

Sophia stood in the doorway, watching the scene unfold. The alarm continued blaring.

"Do you think she's...?" Sophia asked, not wanting to say the dreaded word.

Hank was silent. He laid Hazel's wrist back down on the bed next to her carefully and slowly, and then reached to hit the button on the side of the phone to silence the alarm.

"Ms. Adams, do you have a phone on you, by chance?" Hank asked in a solemn voice, his eyes soft as he turned to look at Sophia.

Sophia managed to confirm that she did, and as she fumbled for it in her purse, Hank said, "Could you please call 911? I'm afraid Hazel is no longer with us."

# Chapter Eight

"Thank you for coming in, Hank," Sheriff Mark Streen said, pushing the blank pad of yellow paper over towards Deputy Chris Jones, sitting beside him.

"Glad to help," Hank said. Hank Davis was an average looking man, with an average height of just under six feet tall and an average build - not muscular, but not too skinny. Leaning back in his seat, he stretched his arms wide and then interlaced his fingers behind his neck in a resting position. "I can't believe Hazel is dead. I think you're gonna find out that it was natural causes. I can't imagine anyone sneaking into my inn and killing some-one. Let alone Hazel."

"We hope you're right. We should get the autopsy report pretty soon," the sheriff said, "but, I want to ask you some questions just in case, you know, to get ahead of things and all if there turns out to be foul play." It was true that there were no autopsy results, but Mark was suspicious. He couldn't place it, but his gut was telling him there was something to be investigated. He had Chris take photos of everything in that room and treat it like a crime scene, just in case. And Hank had agreed to not let anyone touch anything and lock the door to the room at the inn until they found out more.

"So, this is just a casual conversation," Sheriff Streen clarified.

"Right, like old friends," Hank said. Mark thought he might have detected a bit of sarcasm in Hank's voice, and he would only expect that. It wasn't that long ago Mark was knocking on Hank's door, questioning him as a suspect in a previous murder, so he had prepared himself for a smidgeon of contempt from Hank.

The sheriff and deputy exchanged quick glances and Mark continued, ignoring Hank's comment. "So, when was the last time you saw Hazel?"

"Well, I reckon it was at the team meeting yesterday afternoon," Hank said, biting his lip and looking off to the right as he thought about it.

"Who was at the team meeting?" Deputy Chris Jones asked next, pen in hand, ready to record the names of the meeting attendees in his notes.

"The whole crew was there. Me, Hazel, Jonah Troyer, Sebastian Lee, Emily Plankton, and Peggy Fremont." Hank was counting the names using his fingers as he listed them to make sure he didn't forget anyone.

Chris was listing the names on the lines of his paper, then when he finished, he looked up and asked, "What time was the meeting?"

"It started right at 4:00, I think. Peggy was almost late, but she made it there just in time." Hank shook his head, "Man, I'll tell you, Hazel just hated that girl, Peggy." As soon as he finished the sentence, he realized the way it sounded to the two lawmen. He sat up straight and fumbled through his words, "Well, I mean, not hated. Hazel didn't like very many people, I don't think. But it's true that she was downright mean to Peggy sometimes." He ran his hand through his short, thinning light brown hair, and continued, talking quickly. "Before you get any ideas, now, I'm not trying to say Peggy hurt Hazel. Like I said, I think Hazel must've died because of some heart attack or something, but if, by any chance, you find out differently, I don't want it to seem like I'm pointin' my finger at Peggy. She's a good girl. And a hard worker. She wouldn't do anything to hurt anybody."

Chris was taking notes and it was notably making Hank more nervous.

Mark spoke up next, "I know what you meant, Hank. It's ok. Like I said, this isn't a murder investigation yet. And I know Ms. Fremont, too. I wouldn't think she would hurt anyone either." He hoped that agreeing with Hank would help him calm down a bit and continue talking. If there's one thing the sheriff had learned over the years, it was that the more comfortable a person got, the more conversation - and details - they'd share.

Hank let out a loud sigh of relief and relaxed back in his chair. Mark noticed that Chris wrote the word "dramatic" down on his paper and he suppressed a chuckle.

"Ok, so back to the meeting, Hank," Mark said, wanting to continue with the questioning. "So, tell me how the meeting went with everyone. How did it end, in particular?"

Hank thought for a moment and then reluctantly said, "Fine. Nothing really weird. Everybody just got back to work."

Mark cocked his head. Whenever someone went from telling a story with a lot of detail to answering a question with only a few words, and the choice words being things like "fine, nothing happened," he suspected they weren't telling the truth.

"Are you sure?" Mark gave Hank another chance to answer the question.

Hank looked at Mark and said, "Yep," before returning to biting his lip.

"Ok," Mark said. He decided to steer the conversation in a different direction but was glad to see that Chris had written *something happened at the end of the meeting* on the notepad.

"You said Hazel was staying at the inn for a couple nights," Mark said. "Do you know why she wasn't staying at her home on Billings Street?"

Hank shook his head, "No, I really don't. All I know is that she asked if she could stay at the inn for a few nights because of something personal she had going on. Hazel and I didn't talk about personal stuff with each other. But she seemed stressed out and we had an empty room, she said, so I told her it was totally fine. I'm good to my employees like that," Hank said. "If they need something, I give it to 'em."

Chris spoke up with a flat tone, "That's real nice of you, Hank." Again, Mark had to stifle a laugh, so he reached for his bottle of water and took a gulp.

"So, you don't know why Hazel needed a room?" Mark repeated the question, hoping to push Hank a little further.

Hank narrowed his eyes and responded with a sharp "Nope." After a brief pause, he stretched his arms out to his sides and said, "Well, if there's nothing else, I should probably get back. I mean I don't have a manager anymore, you know. I got things to do back at the inn."

"I understand," Mark said, rising to his feet and reaching out his hand as an invitation for a handshake. "We appreciate your time."

Hank stood and shook Mark's hand first then Chris's hand before turning to leave. "You'll let me know what you find out, I guess?" He asked as he reached for the knob on the front door of the small sheriff's office.

"Oh, you'll be the first to know," Mark said, holding the door open for Hank as he walked out onto the porch. "Have a good day, now."

"Yep, same to you fellas," Hank said as he bounded down the steps and jumped into his pickup truck, throwing a wave in the air as he pulled out onto the highway.

Mark shut the door and headed toward the tiny kitchen located just behind his desk. The sheriff's office was once a small house, now transformed into a four-room office with a jail. The jail had only seen a few visitors over the years and was more often empty than occupied.

"Well, what do you think?" Chris asked his mentor. "Do you think we're gonna find out that Hazel died of more than just natural causes?"

"I'm not sure," Mark said, bent overlooking in the small freezer for a snack. "But I have a weird feeling about it."

"Hmm," Chris said. "I don't know. She was pretty young to have heart problems, but it's not unheard of, I guess." He took a drink from the coffee cup sitting on the desk in front of him. "I do think it might be more than a little weird that her door was open. And," he paused briefly before continuing, "I don't know if you noticed, but she looked like she was in the middle of eating her breakfast."

"How do you mean?" Mark responded with his back to Chris as he threw a frozen meal into the microwave and touched the quick start button. The microwave began to hum, and Mark turned around, leaning on the counter.

"Well, I noticed she had one of those pastries from the new bakery on her bedside table, and she had taken a bite out of it. But, really, that's not what's weird. What was weird, is that it looked like she had spit the bite back out into the box. Like it tasted bad or something." Chris said, his hands resting in front of him, fingertips touching to form a triangle.

"That's really interesting, Chris," Mark said, "because I noticed she had some of that white powdered sugar on her lips and even on her shirt." He stopped and the two just stared at each other for a moment, silent.

The microwave stopped humming and beeped. Mark stuffed his hands in his pockets. "Are you thinking what I'm thinking, Chris?"

Chris nodded. "Yep, I think we got us some foul play, Sheriff."

Before Mark could answer, his phone rang. He reached in his pocket and put the phone to his ear. "Sheriff Streen here," he said.

Chris watched, leaning forward in his chair.

"Yes, I understand. Thank you for letting me know."

He nodded at Chris and continued talking, "Yes. So, you're sure then?"

Chris exhaled the breath he had been holding in and shook his head. He removed his cowboy hat and ran his hands through his hair.

Mark ended his phone conversation and set his phone down on the counter next to him. "Well, I guess we have our answer then. The cause of death is acute cyanide poisoning. Ms. Hazel Thompson didn't have a heart attack. I'm afraid she was murdered."

# Chapter Nine

———❖———

"I think that's *gut* enough, *Schwester*," Anna said, trying to remain patient. She and Beth were making a list of the things they would need to host the Schwartz's upcoming homecoming party, and as usual, Anna felt that Beth was taking things a little too far.

"I know, I know. I overthink things a bit, but I really want this to be perfect," Beth said, tapping the pencil on the paper in front of her.

"It *will* be perfect," Anna said. "On that list, you have enough food to feed the entire town of Little Valley, not just our community."

Beth looked at Anna, her eyebrows drawn together, "Do you think it's too much? Maybe we need to take some things off the list." She cast her eyes back down at the long-handwritten list in front of her, her pencil poised to erase something.

Anna laughed lightheartedly, "*Jah*, maybe we can take a few things off the list. Why don't we ask Rachel what foods are her favorites, and we can go from there?" Noticing Beth's mood had changed from excitement to worry, she thought it would be best to shift her attention to something else.

"Let's take a break. Sometimes when you put a project aside and come back to it with a fresh mind, you have more clarity. Besides, remember planning a party is supposed to be fun, not stressful.

"Let's get ready for Sophia's visit, what do you say?" Anna asked, reaching out to collect the pencil and paper from Beth.

Beth reluctantly handed the pencil to her sister and slid the paper away. She let out a loud sigh. "You know how I hate not finishing a project."

Anna tucked the pencil and paper away on the bookshelf and with her back turned to her sister, she responded, "You've done such a *wunderbaar* job on planning the party. Rachel is going to love it. Plus, the planning is practically done. We will make a few small tweaks later, but you can put it to rest in your mind for now."

She turned around to find Beth frowning. "What's the matter, Beth? I feel like you're upset about more than just the party planning not being finished."

Beth stood up and straightened her *kapp*, checking to make sure no strands of hair were loose. "I'm fine, Anna. I guess I'm just a little nervous about Sophia's visit. I wish I knew what to expect. Or at the very least, what *she* is expecting."

Anna walked over and put her arm around Beth's waist, gently coaxing her over to the kitchen area. She knew that the best way for Beth to manage her anxiety was with busy hands, so she grabbed a cutting board and handed Beth a cucumber and a paring knife. "Could you please make your delicious cucumber tomato salad for lunch? That will surely win Sophia over," Anna smiled.

Beth nodded and began to chop the cucumber.

Anna broke the silent tension and tried again to reassure her sister, "Sophia seemed really nice when we met her the other day. I have a *gut* feeling about her. And, I was mostly worried about the photos, but she already agreed to not take pictures, so that's *gut*."

Anna noticed Beth's shoulders began to relax. Setting the table for lunch, Anna continued talking. "It will be very interesting to get to know someone from a big city. And she must be very smart since she's a writer for a magazine."

Beth nodded, "That's true. I guess it will be interesting to get to know her."

Anna pressed her lips in a small smile and took a couple of the fresh white daisies out of the big vase in her living room, cut their stems shorter and placed them in a small vase, setting them in the center of the table.

"*Jah*, and we should feel blessed to have an opportunity to represent the community. She is writing an article in her magazine about us, after all." Anna said.

Beth had moved on to chopping the tomato. She nodded, and said, "*Jah*, but I think that is what is making me most nervous."

Anna set out handmade sandwich rolls, lunch meat and cheese next to a bowl of homemade potato salad that she and Beth had made together earlier. "You don't have to worry, *Schwester*. I'm happy to do most of the talking if you're feeling uncomfortable."

Beth added the freshly made cucumber tomato salad to the table and smiled warmly at her sister, "*Denki*, Anna. I don't know what I would ever do without you."

Anna grabbed Beth's hand and squeezed it. "Well, I feel the same way, *Schwester*. I feel the exact same way."

With perfect timing, a car pulled up to the house and the sisters watched Sophia Adams step out of the car. She appeared to take in the scene for a few moments before walking towards the front porch steps.

"She's here," Anna sang out, making sure to keep her voice light and airy. She headed to the door to greet Sophia and Beth followed closely behind her.

Sophia barely had a chance to knock before Anna opened the heavy wooden front door.

"Welcome!" Anna said as she held the door open wide.

Beth stood next to Anna, her mirror image, smiling, "*Gut* day, Sophia! We're glad you're here."

"*Denki*," Sophia said to both ladies. "Your place is just absolutely beautiful."

"Please do come in," Anna said, and Sophia stepped inside the modest living room. "How has your day been so far?"

Sophia set her purse down on a bench near the door, and said, "Well, it has been eventful. Let's just say that I'm definitely glad to be here."

Beth spoke up, "Well, we've prepared lunch. Would you like to wash your hands and join us for a meal?"

Sophia gratefully accepted the invitation and the three of them settled down at the table. Beth poured sweetened iced tea into each of their glasses and offered a small plate of cut lemons to Sophia. The salad bowls and sandwich platter were passed around until the women each had a full plate. The sisters asked Sophia if she would like to join them in prayer. She nodded, and they bowed their heads for a short prayer of thanks led quietly by Beth.

"So, how are you liking Little Valley so far, Sophia?" Anna asked between bites.

"I'm not sure if this is the right conversation for lunch, but have the two of you heard about what happened this morning at the Amish Inn?" Sophia asked, her sandwich in one hand, her other hand resting in her lap.

The sisters glanced at each other. Beth's son, Jonah, was working at the Amish Inn, but they hadn't spoken with Jonah since his visit for dinner a few days prior - and everything was going well then. Anna knew that she and her sister had the same immediate fears that Jonah might be hurt or in trouble.

"Oh, no," Beth said, setting her fork down with a clatter.

"Do I have permission to speak freely at the lunch table?" Sophia asked, looking at each sister, one at a time. "It feels so much like the elephant in the room, and I want so badly to tell you what has happened."

"Of course," Anna said. "Please do share." She and Beth set full attention on Sophia, leaning forward slightly with anticipation.

"Well, I'm sorry to say that Ms. Hazel Thompson ...she's the manager at the inn you know. She's, um, she has passed away. She's no longer with us." Sophia stumbled through her words.

The sisters both gasped. Anna raised her right hand to her mouth and Beth reached out and grabbed her left hand, holding tight. Beth's face was white. Anna squeezed her hand before turning back to Sophia.

"*Ach du lieva*, this is *baremlich* news. Are you certain? I mean, what happened? Hazel was so young and seemed so healthy." Anna said, feeling Beth's leg start to bounce. She knew that Beth wanted to know about Jonah, but she was careful not to say anything at all considering he hadn't even been mentioned as of yet. She also knew that Beth was thinking the same thing as her. Maybe they were a bit paranoid, but could Hazel have been murdered?

Sophia shook her head. "I know, it's just terrible. Unfortunately, I found her in her room. You guess she was staying at the inn for a couple of nights. Her door was cracked, and her alarm was going off for a while, so I pushed the door open a bit to check on her. She looked like she was sleeping. I called out her name, but..." her voice trailed off.

"I'm so sorry you had to find her like that," Anna said. "I can't imagine what that must've been like."

"*Denki*, but I ran to get help and bumped into Hank, the owner of the inn. And he totally jumped in and took over. He was truly wonderful about everything," Sophia continued. "I'm sure he felt just terrible about all of it."

Beth spoke up, "Sophia, my son, Jonah works there. Do you know if he is ok?"

Sophia nodded, "*Jah*, Jonah is totally fine. I've had the pleasure of meeting your son. He actually was the first one I met in Little Valley. He greeted me at the front door the day I arrived. He is such a nice young man. I had seen from my window earlier ...before I found Hazel ...Jonah and the gardener were out in the yard working."

"Thank *Gotte* he is safe," Beth said, looking at Anna, squeezing her hand gently before releasing it.

Sophia looked a bit confused, so Anna tried to explain. "I just hate that this was your experience in Little Valley. We've had a few crimes lately, and so I think it's probably normal that we would jump right to the worst-case scenario."

Beth nodded, then remembering why Sophia was there, she added, "The last thing we want is for our town to be perceived as dangerous."

The three women returned to eating their lunch, silent for a few moments.

Sophia swallowed a sip of tea and said, "I understand. I promise to try my best at writing my article in a way that describes Little Valley as what it is, a beautiful town, full of really wonderful and kind people.

"Speaking of that, I would love to hear more about your community. Now that the elephant is out of the room, maybe we could talk about something a bit more light-hearted. I would love to take a walk, if you are up for it and hear all about the history, and the growth, of your community."

"*Jah*, we should do that," Anna said, standing to join Beth in clearing the table.

"I could drive us in the buggy," Beth said eagerly. Anna was glad to see that Beth's mood seemed happy once again.

"Hmm... I should warn Sophia that Beth's driving could be an adventure of its own," Anna teased her sister.

"I would love that!" Sophia said. "I trust you, Beth. I can't imagine it could be any worse than driving in a car during rush hour at home." The three women laughed and headed out onto the front porch, Sophia grabbing her purse on the way.

Beth went around the side of the house to bring the horse and buggy to the front, and Anna began to explain how the two sisters shared a few plots of land, their homes built side-by-side. As Beth appeared around the corner, the sheriff's car approached the house. Beth stopped the horse and jumped out of the buggy and stood next to Anna and Sophia.

The car parked in front of the house and Sheriff Mark Streen stepped out of the driver's side. Deputy Chris Jones stepped out of the passenger side just seconds later.

"Howdy, ladies! It's good to see you!" The two lawmen greeted them, almost in unison.

"Well, *hallo*, gentlemen. What brings you two out here today?" Anna asked, waving her hand.

Mark removed his cowboy hat as they got closer and said, "I'm afraid, we're here on business. We were hoping to have a few minutes with you, Sophia. It's about Hazel." He paused briefly before looking at Beth and Anna. "I'm sure you've heard about Hazel?"

The women nodded. "Since you're here to talk to Sophia, I have to ask..." Anna said reluctantly.

Mark and Chris exchanged a quick glance and Mark answered the unspoken question, "Yes, I'm afraid Hazel's death was not due to natural causes."

Anna and Beth didn't have to exchange more than a shared look to know that they were thinking the exact same thing. As the amateur sleuths in town, things would surely get pretty hectic in their lives in the next few days.

# Chapter Ten

---◄◊►---

E va turned the ovens to preheat and took another
sip of her coffee. She was exhausted after a night
of tossing and turning. Yesterday's sales had taken a
dramatic dip. Her once busy bakery shop now felt like
a ghost town. Word had spread across the town that the
manager at the Amish Inn was found dead, poisoned.
And the worst part was that there was a pastry found in
the victim's room - and it was one of the popular cream
horns from Sugar on Top.

No one wanted to visit the bakery anymore, even though it wasn't yet proven that the pastry contained the poison.

Eva wasn't even sure what she should bake this morning to prepare for the day, and she was at a complete loss on how to save her shop's reputation.

"Good morning," Peggy said cheerfully, as she hung her purse on the hook on the back wall and grabbed a hair net from the box at the end of the counter. She walked over to the sink to wash her hands.

"Morning," Eva muttered. "You seem bright and cheery today." Eva winced at how disgruntled her words sounded.

Peggy dried her hands and got to work kneading the dough waiting for her on the worktable. Each morning, Eva would get there early and take the dough out of the refrigerator, preparing for it to be at room temperature by the time Peggy arrived. Peggy started every day that she worked at Sugar on Top expertly kneading and separating the dough for the different types of pastries that it would become.

"I guess I did sleep well last night," Peggy said. "I'm sorry, though. You don't look like you're feeling too good. Is everything ok? I know we didn't have very many customers yesterday, but I really do think this will pass, Eva." She talked quickly, full of energy.

"I certainly hope it does and sooner than later, too." Eva said, sounding less than hopeful. "You're right, though. I'm not feeling too *gut*. I just can't figure out how this all could've happened, and I didn't sleep well last night."

"I'm not gonna lie. With her being gone, my life has already been so much easier, and less horrible." Peggy said, referring to Hazel. "But" she continued, "I do agree that it's a terrible coincidence that she had a pastry from Sugar on Top in her room. I wish it could have been different, for sure." Peggy said, sympathizing with Eva.

Eva turned away from Peggy as she fought back tears. She headed to the bathroom at the back of the store to compose herself. Leaning on the sink and looking in the mirror, she thought to herself, *you've got to pull it together, Eva. Everything is going to be ok.*

She splashed cold water on her face and took a deep breath in, exhaling slowly. She was going to have to figure out how to get out of this mess, and she would need a clear head - and controlled emotions - to do so. She knew that she could rely on her cousins Anna and Beth to help get to the bottom of this, and she took comfort in knowing they were on her side.

Returning to the kitchen, she found Peggy placing her filled sheet pans into the ovens.

"Ok," Eva said, "Let's see. What should we prepare next?"

Peggy responded, "I am putting the cream horns in the oven now. Up next is the breakfast muffins and friendship bread."

"Perfect," Eva said. "Thank you. I'll get started on the bread if you want to tackle the muffins."

"Sure!" Peggy said, reaching for a mixing bowl and starting to collect the ingredients. After a few minutes of working side by side in silence, Peggy spoke, "I'm sorry if I upset you, Eva."

Eva continued working and responded, "What do you mean, Peggy? I'm not upset with you. It's this whole thing. I'm going to continue to pray for answers and for the person who is responsible for Hazel's death to be found. Once that happens, Sugar on Top will get back to normal."

Peggy was quiet as she added a cup of sugar to the egg mixture in front of her.

"My cousins, Anna and Beth, are going to be asking around and trying to get to the bottom of all of this. And of course, the sheriff and the deputy are on the case, too. It will only be a matter of time before the truth comes out," Eva said as she rubbed a stick of butter along the insides of the bread pans.

Peggy grabbed another mixing bowl and measured out flour, baking soda and salt. She began mixing the dry ingredients, without a word.

"How is it at the inn now? I know you said your life is easier now, but how are Hank Davis and the rest of the staff holding up there? Are they experiencing a lul in business?" Eva asked Peggy.

"Actually, no, there seems to be a high demand for wanting the yellow room now. That's the room Hazel was found in. It has bright yellow paint on the walls and was always my favorite before all of this happened.

"I guess some people really like to visit places where people were killed. They think it might be haunted or something. It's weird, I know.

"Hank is actually a really nice guy, but he is also all about business, and somehow this turned out to be good for business. So, he's happy. We're all working really hard, though. More customers means more to clean, and more for Emily to cook. Jonah and Sebastian have been working on outdoor projects mainly. Hank is filling in for Hazel, checking everyone in and out and booking the stays. That's overwhelming for him, though." Peggy paused briefly before continuing.

"He actually said that he's thinking about training me to do the management stuff. I was going to talk to you about that." Peggy started talking faster. "So, it would mean more money for me, but it would also mean that I had to work earlier hours at the inn. And with things slowing down here, well, it might work out really well, I was thinking." Peggy took a deep breath.

Eva stopped before pouring the cake batter into the pans and turned to look at Peggy. "I'm not sure what to say," Eva hesitated. "I mean, I'd be happy for you to have an opportunity like that. It sounds like a promotion?" Eva raised her voice at the end of her last sentence turning it into a question.

Peggy nodded.

Eva continued, "Of course, I don't expect things to be slow here for long, like I said. Once we find out who is behind this, I think business will return to normal here." She paused, waiting for Peggy to respond.

"Oh, sure. Yeah. Of course," Peggy stuttered and avoided eye contact as she headed toward the sink to wash her mixing bowl after pouring the batter into the muffin pans. "Realistically, though, that could take a while. I mean Hazel was not a nice person. I can only assume that the list of suspects must be really long."

Eva was stunned. She had never seen this side of Peggy. Something felt off, and she was unnerved. It felt as if Peggy was not only glad that Hazel was dead, but she also didn't seem too concerned about the future of Sugar on Top. Eva shook it off. She knew that Peggy was a genuinely nice person. She must be overthinking it.

"Well, regardless of whether Sugar on Top gets busy again or not, Peggy, I want you to do whatever makes you the happiest. It's great that Hank is considering you for the management job, and I'll support whatever you need to do." Eva said, checking in on the cream horns and placing the muffin pans and bread pans in the other oven.

Peggy shut off the water and turned around, leaning on the counter next to the sink. "Thank you so much, Eva. I knew you would understand. Nothing is official yet, so I'll keep you posted. And I am hoping that I can still help with your morning prep as long as you need the help."

A knock at the door interrupted the conversation. Eva looked up and said, "Oh! The sheriff and deputy are here. I forgot to tell you they were coming by. They want to ask some questions since they found our pastry in Hazel's room."

"Oh," Peggy said before turning back around and returning to the task of washing the prep dishes from that morning.

Eva walked to the front door and welcomed the two lawmen into her shop. She locked the door behind them since it was still too early to open the shop.

"Can I get you men some coffee? We should have some muffins cooked soon, too, if you're hungry. They're in the oven now so they'll be nice and hot." Eva said, gesturing for Mark and Chris to have a seat at the table in the center of the dining area.

Mark spoke, "Thank you, coffee and warm muffins sound wonderful." Chris agreed.

"Could you pour a couple cups of hot coffee, please, Peggy?" Eva called out to the back before settling down in a seat across from the men.

"Oh, Peggy's here?" Mark asked.

"Yes, she works with me Tuesdays through Saturdays. She's a huge help around here." Eva said.

Peggy came around from behind the counter with two cups of steaming hot coffee, a few packs of sugar and a small pitcher of cream. Setting it down, she said hello to the men politely.

"Thank you, Peggy," Eva said, and the men thanked her, as well.

"Why don't you join us, Peggy?" Mark said, as she had turned to walk away.

Stopping in her tracks and slowly turning back toward the group, Peggy said, "Oh, thank you, Sheriff, but I couldn't. I have to check on the cooking. And I have some cream horns to fill and cookies to decorate." She turned back to head towards the kitchen, when this time, it was Eva that spoke.

"Peggy," Eva said, and Peggy stopped in her tracks. Her shoulders creeped toward her ears. "Could you please bring the men some muffins when they're ready?"

Peggy nodded, her hands clasped together tightly in front of her.

"Wait, before you go, Peggy," Mark said. "I mean, I don't want anything to burn, of course, but I think you both need to hear this." He looked at Chris, and Chris nodded.

"It's important that you both know that forensics testing came back and the pastry that was found in Hazel's room had a layer of cyanide poison on top. It could easily have looked like sugar, but it was poison. That's what killed Hazel. It was actually the cream horn." As Mark's words rolled out of his mouth, Eva felt a tear escape from her eye and run down her cheek.

"Oh, no," Eva whispered. "But how...?"

Peggy dropped her hands by her side, "Are you sure? I mean, could there be some kind of mistake with the tests?" She asked, her voice cracking.

Chris spoke first, "It's not likely that the tests are wrong. The numbers from the test were really high, and it didn't take much of a bite for Hazel to die from the poison. So, I guess there was quite a bit of poison on that pastry."

Eva shook her head and then, catching a whiff of the baked goods in the oven, she said in a flat tone, "Peggy, could you please go check on the food in the oven?"

Peggy looked relieved. She nodded and ran off to check on the cream horns, muffins, and bread that were baking.

Eva turned to Mark and said, "What do you need from me? How can I help you find who did this?"

Mark took a sip of his coffee and said, "I hate to do it, but I think we're gonna need to start with a search of the ingredients in your kitchen, Ms. Zook."

Eva nodded. Something told her she was going to need to talk to her cousins sooner rather than later.

As she rose to her feet to lead the way to the kitchen, she silently prayed again for the strength to get through this day.

# Chapter Eleven

———◆———

Hank pulled up to the inn and parked in his dedicated parking spot. It was the closest parking space with the only exception being the handicapped space he was required to offer. He had purchased a sign that read *The Boss Parks Here* in large letters with *Park at Your Own Risk* in smaller letters below. Most days, he would chuckle to himself when he pulled into the spot, but he hardly gave it any notice today. His mind was still racing since the sheriff had told him that the autopsy showed that Hazel was poisoned.

He stepped out of the truck and then turned around, leaning back in to grab the paper bag of groceries off the passenger side seat. Emily had a short list of things she needed, and he promised to pick them up while he was out.

"Hey there, Hank!" Sebastian called out from the depths of the overgrown front landscaping.

Hank slammed his truck door shut and waved with his free hand. "How's it goin'? It's startin' to look decent out here."

"Thanks, man. I've been workin' hard. I can't tell you how much I appreciate the opportunity to do this work. I love working outside, and I am enjoying working with you and the rest of the crew. Well, now that, you know..." He winked at Hank.

Hank immediately felt uncomfortable and grimaced. It was too soon to be hearing things like someone was glad that Hazel was gone. "Ah, c'mon man. She wasn't that bad. She did a lot of work around here herself, you know. She was a big part of the whole grand opening being so successful. And honestly, now that she's gone, I am realizing just how much she did. Trust me."

Sebastian shrugged. "I guess you haven't had enough time to figure it out yet."

"What are you talkin' about, Sebastian?" Hank was intrigued but he was also getting a bit irritated with Sebastian's lack of respect for the dead.

Sebastian stood there, silent. He was covered in dirt, his khaki cargo shorts covered in grime, and his navy t-shirt stained and stretched out. His long black hair was tied back and pushed under an ill-fitting cap, strings of hair framing his tanned face.

"You know I'm forever in debt to you, Hank, for giving me a chance and hiring me. I had gone months without finding a job. I was starting to think there was no hope until I met you." Sebastian pushed his hat off his head and swept his hair back, smoothing it down before refitting the hat back on top.

Hank sensed there was something Sebastian wasn't telling him. "I told you, man. You don't have to keep thanking me. I get it. Yeah, I gave you a chance, but you've proven yourself. You work hard, and you're trustworthy."

Sebastian interrupted him. "See, it's interesting you used that word, Hank. Trustworthy."

"Quit talkin' riddles, man, and get to the point. What are you tryin' to say?" Hank shifted the grocery bag from one hip to the other.

"Alright, I'll just say it since you can't see it. Hazel. She wasn't trustworthy, Hank." Sebastian said.

"What?!" Hank was shocked to hear Sebastian say this. "What are you gettin' at? She cheatin' on her boyfriend or somethin'? Did you have a crush on her, Sebastian?" He suspected something like that might be going on since, on a couple occasions, Hank had walked up and caught the two of them in hushed conversations that ended abruptly when they saw him.

"Heck, no!" Sebastian said, looking embarrassed. "You gotta be kiddin' me, Hank." He scoffed. "Don't ya think I could do better than that scrawny mean girl?"

Hank flinched as Sebastian threw another blow at Hazel. Hank thought to himself that truthfully, he thought Hazel would actually be out of Sebastian's league, but he decided against saying that out loud.

"Please get to the point before the ice cream in this bag melts," Hank said, anxious to end this conversation and move on with his long to-do list.

"Hazel was stealing from you, Hank," Sebastian blurted out. "There, I finally said it"

Hank's mouth dropped open. He was speechless.

Sebastian continued, "I kept wondering when you were gonna see it. I figured at some point that maybe you was turnin' a blind eye to it."

Hank shook his head slowly. He had no idea that Hazel was stealing from him. "How do you know?" was all he could mutter.

"I caught her. I saw her doing it. I confronted her about it, and she offered to give me some of it to keep my mouth shut." Sebastian continued with a softer tone.

"I am shocked," Hank said. He wasn't sure if he should believe it or not, but he had noticed that the books weren't matching the bank account balance. He had even questioned Hazel about it a few times, and she had responded with some explanation about deposits that just hadn't hit yet or unexpected expenses that had come up. Hank knew he needed to be more in control of everything, but he totally trusted Hazel when she said that the profit was coming. For some reason, it made perfectly good sense to him that there wouldn't be much profit at the start of opening a business, so he didn't really question her.

"Well, I'm sorry to be the bearer of bad news, but it's true. She was a thief. And she was about to take this whole place down. Then we'd all be out of work, and you'd have to shut down the inn... and all because she was fillin' up her own pockets." Sebastian said, shaking his head, his hands clenched next to his sides. "I still get so angry thinkin' about it. She said she was gonna stop, but she kept doin' it."

Hank set the groceries down on the bottom step next to him and leaned on the railing of the porch. "So, let me just get this straight. You're tellin' me that Hazel was stealin' from me... on the regular."

Sebastian nodded. "Yep."

Hank sighed and ran his hand through his hair. "Well, I'll be damned," he muttered. Letting it soak in, Hank realized this was really not good. It wasn't good for the inn's cash flow, sure, but it wasn't going to look good to the police either if they found it. They could easily pin this on him as a motive for Hazel's death. He looked at Sebastian who just stood there staring back at him, waiting for him to think it all through before saying another word.

"Sebastian," Hank began slowly, his voice lowered. "Who else knows about this?"

Sebastian hesitated before responding, "About her stealin'? As far as I know, we're the only ones who know about it." After a brief pause, Sebastian began talking quickly, "Hank, you know I didn't cut no deal with her, right? You know I wouldn't do that, right, Hank? I never took none of what she was offering me to shut my mouth. I promise you. I didn't want no part of takin' advantage of you, Hank."

Hank jumped into caretaker mode. "Oh, I know, Sebastian. I know you would never do that. You and I are like family, right? I mean, I consider you like a brother to me."

A wide smile spread across Sebastian's face. "Aw, thanks, Hank. That's the best thing you coulda said. I feel like that, too."

Hank continued, satisfied with Sebastian's response. "So, you know, we can't tell anyone about this, right? Even though Hazel is dead. We don't want to tell anyone at all about her stealing. Can you keep it our little secret, Sebastian? You know, like a secret between brothers?"

Sebastian stood tall and saluted Hank as if to show loyalty and honor. "Sure thing, Hank. It'll be our secret. No worries at all. I'm just glad it's all over now, and I don't have to worry about ya anymore."

Hank smiled. "Well, I do appreciate ya lookin' out for me, Sebastian. Now, I've spent enough time hangin' out. I gotta get back to work and make some more money." He said with a wink.

Sebastian grinned and winked back, "Alright, yeah, that's a good idea, Hank. I'll catch ya later, brother."

Hank grabbed the paper bag off the bottom step and headed up the porch steps.

As he reached the top step, Sebastian called out, "Oh, hey, one more thing, Hank. I spotted some critters out close to the house since I've been removing all the dead bushes and all. I bought some stuff to put down in the crawlspace that should take care of the problem. The pesticide stuff can kill more than just field mice, though, so if it's ok with you, I'd like to put some chicken wire along the foundation to keep any stray cats and dogs safe."

Hank waved his arm in the air, "Yeah, sure. Whatever you need to do, Sebastian. Thanks, man."

He opened the door to the inn, closing it behind him as he entered.

Peggy was in the front room, cleaning the picture window that looked out over where he and Sebastian just had their conversation. She had her back turned toward the door when he first walked in, bent down to pick up the cleaner. When she stood, Hank had already passed her and was standing a couple feet behind her. He paused for a minute, wondering if she overheard any of the conversation.

"Hey, Peggy," he said.

Peggy didn't answer.

Hank could hear a faint sound of high-pitched music. It only took him a few seconds to realize that Peggy was listening to earphones. She didn't hear him say hello, so she definitely couldn't have overheard the conversation outside.

With a sigh of relief, Hank headed to the kitchen to give Emily the bag of groceries. Then, he wanted to hole up in his office and take a closer look at his books before anyone else did.

# Chapter Twelve

⸻

Anna held on tight to the handle affixed to the ceiling of Beth's buggy. "Please be careful, Beth," Anna begged.

Beth rolled her eyes. "You're so dramatic, Anna. Are you ever going to forget that one wreck we were in? You know that was a special situation. Besides, Noah says I'm a *gut* driver."

"I will not forget," Anna said. "And special situation or not, you drive a little too fast for my taste. I would like to arrive at Heaven's Diner in one piece."

"I will get you there safely, *Schwester*, I promise," Beth said with a smile.

The sisters enjoyed a comfortable silence the last two miles to the diner. Anna's mind was spinning. Eva had relayed her conversation with the sheriff and deputy at the bakery the day before. Even though the lawmen did not find anything poisonous in Eva's kitchen during their search, Anna was concerned for Eva's future. It certainly did not look good that the weapon used to kill Hazel was a poisoned pastry that resembled the very popular cream horns from Sugar on Top.

Beth parked the horse and buggy in front of the diner and the two women headed inside. They were delivering a box of cinnamon rolls to the owner, Jessica McLean. Jessica purchased weekly orders of the cinnamon rolls to stock her case and sell to her customers. Since most of the townsfolk knew that Eva was Anna and Beth's cousin, Anna was anxious to hear if the cinnamon rolls were continuing to sell in the diner despite the town's wariness to eat at Sugar on Top.

The chime on the door dinged as Anna and Beth entered. The diner was empty, but Anna knew that it would be buzzing with customers in the next hour, all hungry for lunch. Jessica was behind the counter, emptying her dishwasher. She smiled big when she saw the sisters walk in the front door.

"Hello, Anna and Beth! I was hoping to see you today!" Jessica called out.

"*Hallo*, Jessica!" Anna and Beth returned the greeting in unison.

"Please come in and have a seat. Your timing is perfect. I can join you for a cup of coffee and a chat before lunch hits, if you have time to visit for a few minutes." Jessica gingerly touched the coffee carafe sitting on the coffeemaker to see if it was still hot from the last brew.

Anna and Beth exchanged glances to see if the other had an objection before agreeing to stay and visit. They nodded to each other, and Beth responded, "Sure! We would love a cup of coffee. Thank you!"

They headed to their favorite booth, situated on the far right of the large wall of windows at the front of the diner. It looked out over Main Street, across from Moses's hardware store and Matthew's flower shop. The women enjoyed people watching and they had determined years ago that this was the best booth in the diner for that.

Jessica brought over coffee cups filled with hot coffee and a small container holding packets of raw sugar. "Sugar, no cream, right?" She asked, knowing the answer.

"*Jah*, thank you." Anna said, smiling. She passed one of the cups to Beth who was sitting on her right.

Jessica returned the carafe to the coffeemaker and then hurried back to the booth with a cup of her own and sat down in the booth across from Anna and Beth. The sun looked as if it were pointed directly toward her, causing the curly locks of her strawberry blonde hair to look more red than normal. Her face had a tanned a bit over the summer months which accentuated and brightened her green eyes.

Beth slid the box of cinnamon rolls toward Jessica.

"Oh, thank you so much," Jessica said. "Your timing is perfect on this."

Anna asked, "So you're still selling the cinnamon rolls? I was wondering if the town might be on strike for our baked goods, as well as Eva's."

"Oh, no. I don't have any problem selling these cinnamon rolls. They are a fan favorite around here, and the tourists really love them." Jessica said. She took a sip of her coffee before approaching the subject of what was going on with Eva. "I'm so sorry that this has happened to Eva. Unfortunately, I do hear a lot of people talking about it. Hopefully, it will blow over soon and just be a thing of the past."

Anna and Beth nodded.

"*Jah*, we hope for the same," Beth said. "It's terrible what happened to Hazel Thompson."

"And terrible that Eva has been dragged into this, for sure," Anna agreed.

Jessica nodded, "It's unfortunate for everyone, except for Olivia Black." She rolled her eyes. "That woman seems to be very happy about all of it. Business has picked up for her over at Something Sweet."

"I'm sure it has," Beth said under her breath.

The door chime could be heard and all three of the women looked as Sheriff Mark Streen and Deputy Chris Jones entered the diner.

"Well, I thought that might be your buggy sitting out there!" Mark said in a loud boisterous voice.

The women all smiled and exchanged greetings with the men.

"Pull up some chairs and join us," Jessica said, gesturing for the men to grab chairs from the nearby table. "Can I get you guys some coffee?"

"That'd be great," Chris was the first to respond.

"I'll take one of those cinnamon rolls, too," Mark added, and Chris agreed and asked for one, as well.

"Coming right up," Jessica said as she headed to the counter to grab their orders.

"How are you doing today?" Beth asked Mark and Chris, making small talk as they waited for their coffee.

Anna could feel the mood shift from cheery to concerned before either of the men could even answer.

"Things have been better, for sure," Mark replied. "We were going to stop by your houses later today to chat, but when we saw your buggy parked outside, we decided to come on in and catch you here instead."

Beth grabbed Anna's hand under the table, and Anna gently squeezed.

The door chime sounded again and a family of four entered and sat at a table across the diner, out of earshot. Jessica welcomed them and said she would be right with them.

"We can only assume what this important conversation must be about," Anna said to Mark and Chris. Chris nodded. Jessica arrived with the men's coffee and cinnamon rolls and excused herself, promising she would be right back. She told Mark and Chris to make themselves at home in the booth sitting across from the twins, and they did so, placing their chairs back at the table they had pulled them from.

The door chimed again, and this time, Sophia Adams entered the diner. She spotted the sisters and the sheriff and deputy and waved, calling out, "Hello!"

The sisters waved back and returned the warm greeting. She sat down at the counter and began busying herself looking at the lunch menu.

Mark asked, lowering his voice, "So what do you think of Ms. Sophia Adams, the travel journalist?"

Anna and Beth nodded. Beth said, "We really like her. It's just such a shame that she had to find poor Hazel during her stay here. And it doesn't necessarily paint Little Valley in a good light either."

Anna continued, "*Jah*, but she said she wasn't going to focus on that in her article. She was more interested in finding out about the Amish history and about our community and life here in Little Valley instead. So, that was a relief."

The door chime sounded again and an older couple entered the diner, grabbing the booth on the far left on the picture window. Jessica was standing at the table with the family, taking their order, and she called out a greeting to the couple, inviting them to make themselves at home. She glanced over at Anna and Beth's booth and mouthed the word "Sorry" to which Anna waved her hand in the air as if to tell her not to worry about it.

Beth spoke, "The anticipation is *baremlich*. What is it that you wanted to talk to us about, Sheriff?"

Mark nodded and set his coffee cup down. "My apologies. As you probably suspected, it's about Hazel's death. I'm sure you've had a chance to talk to Eva?"

The sisters nodded.

"Well, the problem that we have is that it has been determined that Hazel was killed. She was poisoned. The pastry that killed her had poison all over it, and it was one of those cream puff things sitting in a box from Eva's shop." Mark continued.

"Now, I'm sure the next test results we're gonna get will be fingerprint analysis, and something tells me that there is a good chance Eva's fingerprints are gonna be on that box. And, when that comes back, we'll be in a real pickle because that's the only evidence we have." As he spoke, Mark's eyes were intense, his face serious.

Anna interjected, "You don't believe Eva would do this, though, right?" She looked straight at Mark and squeezed Beth's hand again.

Mark didn't answer. "I have been in this business long enough to know better than to rule just about anyone out."

"But what would be her motive?" Beth asked.

Mark took another sip of his coffee. "Well, that's ultimately why we haven't arrested her yet. That's the missing piece, but if a fingerprint analysis comes back and shows her prints, which I'm pretty confident will happen, then that's when we'll have to move forward."

"She has been very cooperative," Chris chimed in. "She even came in and gave us her fingerprints."

"Which is the reason why we're here," Mark said. "My gut tells me it's not Eva, but we need your help. Talk to Jonah and Eva. Do your sleuthing. Come up with a motive for someone else and help us figure this one out. We'll be working on it, too. We plan to interview Hank some more and the rest of the staff, but you two are quite good at getting to the bottom of a crime in your own way."

It was Beth's turn to squeeze Anna's hand, and Anna felt Beth's knee start to bounce.

Mark took his last bite of cinnamon roll and a gulp of coffee before saying, "But be careful. I can't have anything happen to either of you, and remember, there is a killer out there that doesn't want to be found. That's never a good thing. Watch your back and call us if you need anything."

The two women agreed to help.

He slid out of the booth and Chris followed behind him. Before leaving, Mark said, "Let's keep in touch. How about we meet at the office in a couple days?"

"That sounds good," Anna said, and Beth agreed.

The men headed out the door and passed Matthew coming in. He was carrying a small bouquet of flowers but shook hands with Mark and Chris with his free hand.

The sisters released each other's hand and simultaneously leaned back in the booth.

"*Gut daag*, Anna and Beth!" Matthew called out before approaching their booth. "*Wie bischt?*"

"*Gut daag*, Matthew," the sisters said in unison. "We're well. How are you?" Anna asked.

"Very *gut*. Just here for some lunch," Matthew said.

"Those are beautiful flowers," Beth said, with a knowing smile.

"*Denki, jah*. I brought them for Jessica to set on her counter." Matthew said, his cheeks turning a light shade of pink.

Both sisters grinned and Anna said, "Well, she will love them, I'm sure. See you Sunday night for dinner?"

"*Jah*, I wouldn't miss it. *Denki* for always including me." Matthew said with a grin. "I should run and place my order. I'll see you ladies on Sunday night."

"See you then!" Beth and Anna said.

Once the women were alone again, Anna turned to Beth, "Well, we should probably head out, too. It looks like we've got a busy schedule as well, now."

They dropped a five-dollar bill on the table for Jessica and waved goodbye, reminding her that the box of cinnamon rolls was sitting on the table and promising to see her again soon. They climbed into the buggy and were just about to pull away when they saw Sophia Adams running up to them, waving her arm.

"Wait!" Sophia called out.

The sisters smiled and said, "*Hallo*, Sophia!"

Sophia was out of breath, "I'm so glad I caught you! I couldn't help but overhear what the sheriff said to you about Eva. I think I may be able to help. I know that Hazel was fighting with her boyfriend, and I think Hank might know more than he's saying, too."

The sisters looked at each other and without saying another word, Anna scooted over to make room for Sophia. The three of them headed toward the Amish Inn to start their investigation.

# Chapter Thirteen

---

Beth parked the buggy in the Amish Inn parking lot. The twins and Sophia walked up the porch steps, exchanging brief, but polite, greetings with Sebastian who was working in the front yard as they passed by him. They entered the front sitting room that was designed to resemble an Amish living room. Beth remembered how much she didn't care for this place, mostly for its attempt at imitation and lack of authenticity, but she was grateful that Jonah felt comfortable here with his job as the inn's handyman.

Hank was standing within sight, and he appeared to be teaching the ropes of setting appointments to Peggy Fremont. "So, then you'll get a confirmation email here when the room has been booked, and you can find all of the customer's details back in this software over here," Hank said, as he stood close to Peggy and held an electronic tablet in his hand. Beth wasn't sure why, but it struck her as odd hearing and seeing Hank in a formal work environment. She was surprised to see he was more hands-on with the business than she thought.

Peggy nodded, "Oh, yes, okay. That's easy enough."

Hank looked up as he saw the three women approaching. "Well, hey there. I see that you've met the famous Beth and Anna, Sophia. I figured that was only a matter of time." He grinned.

"*Hallo*, Hank," Anna said. "How are you?"

"Oh, you know, I'm hangin' in there," Hank answered. Beth understood that he was referring to the absence of Hazel without coming right out and saying it. "I'm trainin' Peggy here on some of the management stuff now."

Peggy beamed, wearing a wide smile.

"Oh, congratulations, Peggy," Beth said.

Anna chimed in. "I'm sure she's the perfect one for that job, Hank," she said with a warm smile directed at Peggy.

Beth and Anna thought highly of Peggy. She was a hard worker, and she had been a huge help at Eva's bakery ever since it opened. Beth had been praying for her, and she was so glad to see that she was getting promoted at the inn.

"What can I do for you ladies?" Hank asked, handing the tablet to Peggy and stepping forward. "Are you looking for Jonah?"

"Oh, no. We're actually here to ask you a favor," Anna said. Beth felt butterflies in her stomach.

Hank raised one eyebrow and said, "Oh? Why don't you join me in my office?" And he led the way before waiting for an answer. The sisters and Sophia followed close behind.

Hank's office was very small. All four people barely fit in there, but they managed to squeeze in and shut the door. Hank stood behind his desk and the three women stood together, shoulder to shoulder, on the other side of the desk, facing him.

"So, what's the big favor?" Hank asked, his tone was light, and it sounded to Beth like he wanted to help.

"Well, I'm sure you have figured out by now that our cousin, Eva, is being framed for murdering Hazel since it was her pastry that was poisoned." Anna got right to the point.

Hank nodded slowly, "Ok, I hadn't heard that exactly, but it makes sense."

Beth was feeling more comfortable, so she stepped in and said, "We're trying to clear her name. She didn't do it. She had no motive to kill Hazel, and we're trying to find out who did."

Beth thought she noticed a difference in Hank's demeanor. He stopped making eye contact and started to absent-mindedly gather papers into stacks on his desk.

Anna continued where Beth left off, "So, we're wondering if you happen to have Hazel's boyfriend's contact information? We thought we could at least ask him some questions."

Sophia interjected, "Yes, I heard Hazel and him fighting over the phone as well as in person at the diner before she died. He could be the one behind the murder."

Beth winced. She hadn't really wanted to tell Hank all of that, but it was out there now.

Hank lifted his head and stuttered, "Well, of course, if you think he did it, then for sure, I want to help." He paused briefly before asking, "But why would I have his contact information?"

"Maybe he's listed as her emergency contact on her employee file?" Sophia suggested with a shrug.

"Ah! That's a good point. I have that here somewhere." Then, as Hank started rifling through his file cabinet behind his desk, he muttered, "One second."

A few moments of quiet passed before Hank exclaimed, "Aha!" and pulled a file out of the cabinet, setting it down on his desk. Sure enough, Hazel had Rick Storm listed as her emergency contact and his address matched her main address on the employee information form. That had to be him!

"I think I know exactly where this is," Beth said. She recognized the name of the street as one she passes on the way to the town's library.

Sophia jotted down his name and address and thanked Hank for his help. As they headed out the door, Hank called out, "Good luck, ladies! Keep me posted, will ya?"

Anna, Beth, and Sophia rushed out of the inn, jumped in Beth's buggy, and were on their way within minutes.

Beth, keeping her eyes on the road, said, "Ok, before we get there, can we talk about what we know about this guy? I mean, I think it'd be good if we knew what we were walking into before we got there."

Anna agreed and turned to Sophia, "Tell us everything you know, Sophia."

Sophia didn't hesitate, "Well, I will admit that I don't know much. When Hazel was on the phone with him, it sounded like she was demanding he move out, and he was pushing back on that a bit. Then, when I saw them in the diner, Hazel was very upset and the only thing that really stuck with me was that he pushed the bill towards her and said that she could afford to pay it and he couldn't, or something like that."

Beth responded, "Ok, so it was a breakup, and they could've been having money issues. Was he raising his voice at Hazel at the diner?"

Sophia thought about it and replied, "No, I only remember Hazel raising her voice, now that you mention it."

Anna chimed in. "Well, that's a good sign," she said.

They arrived at the house a few minutes later and parked on the street. Beth jumped out and tied the horse to one of the trees between the sidewalk and the road. She took a deep breath. Butterflies had returned to her stomach.

Anna grabbed an arm on each woman and pulled them both close. "What's our game plan?" She whispered the question as if other people were within hearing range.

Sophia said, "If you want, I can ask the questions. I'm the reporter in the group. It's kinda my job."

Both women eagerly agreed to the plan, and the three of them headed down the front path to the door. They rang the doorbell and heard a large dog bark followed by footsteps headed their way. The door opened and a lanky young man, in his mid-to-late twenties stood before them with a surprised look on his face.

"Oh, I thought you were delivering my dinner," he said. A golden retriever sat down casually next to him.

Sophia jumped into action, "Hi, I'm Sophia Adams. I'm with a national magazine based in Chicago. Are you Rick Storm?"

Rick looked confused and Beth noticed he had bags under his eyes. "Yes, that's me, but I don't have anything to say. No comment, I guess," he said as he started to close the door and turn away.

"Wait," Sophia said. "I'm not actually here for the magazine. I'm the one who found Hazel dead."

The door stopped moving, and Rick slowly turned back around to face the women. "Ok?" he said, returning to that confused look he had previously.

Beth spoke up, "We just wanted to see if you could help us put some of the pieces together around what may have happened. You see, we think our cousin is being framed for Hazel's murder, and we want to help her..."

Anna interrupted her sister, taking half a step forward. "But we also want to find out the truth for Hazel's sake."

Rick's face softened.

"Can we just ask you a few questions?" Sophia asked. "We won't take much of your time."

Rick nodded reluctantly. "Ok, but my house is a wreck. Can you just meet me around back on the patio? The side gate is unlocked."

The women agreed and headed around the side of the house to find a lovely back patio decorated with pots full of blooming flowers. There was an iron table with four matching cushioned chairs set in the center with an umbrella for shade. A hand painted yard decoration of a family of owls sat in the center of the table.

Rick came out the back door as the women came around the side of the house.

"This is beautiful," Sophia remarked.

"Thank you," Rick said. "I spend a lot of time out here. It's kind of my happy place. I like to garden." He said shyly.

The four chose chairs and sat down.

"So, what kind of questions did you have for me? How can I help?" Rick asked, his elbows propped on the table, his fingers interlaced in front of him.

Anna began, "Well, let's just get right to it. Do *you* know who would've wanted Hazel dead?"

Rick rubbed the back of his neck and leaned back in his chair. "Unfortunately, the only one that makes sense to me is her boss, Hank Davis."

Beth stifled a gasp but shared the same surprised look as her sister. She was not expecting that answer, and she was pretty sure Anna wasn't either.

Rick continued, "Uh, yeah. Hazel was stealing money from the Amish Inn. She had a real problem with it. She started out just taking a little bit here and there, but then she got more and more greedy. I'm thinking he must've found out about and killed her." He paused, and since neither of the women responded, he confirmed, "So... like I said, that's the only thing that makes sense to me."

Anna and Beth looked at each other. They had no idea that Hazel was stealing money from Hank. Was Rick's intuition right? Could Hank have killed Hazel?

# Chapter Fourteen

---

Beth sat at Anna's table, her knee bouncing under the table. She didn't sleep very well after their visit with Hazel's boyfriend, Rick Storm. It was all she could do to not try to stop Jonah from going to work today. She worried terribly that he might not be safe.

Anna set a fresh cup of coffee in front of Beth and sat down across the table from her. She grabbed a pad of paper that she had stashed in the bookcase. The front page contained all of Beth's notes for the Schwartz's homecoming party. She flipped the page to a clean sheet and grabbed the pencil that Beth was using to drum nervously on the table.

"Ok, let's get our thoughts together here," said Anna. "We have talked about so much. I think it might help if we write it down."

Beth agreed and took a sip of her coffee. "Let's start with Hank," she said, crossing her arms in front of her. "I think he's our prime suspect right now."

Anna wrote *Hank Davis* in neatly printed letters and then next to Hank's name, she wrote *Hazel was stealing from the inn.* She looked up and paused.

After a few minutes, she wrote *Rick Storm*. Beth was watching her sister print the letters. She said aloud, "*Jah*, I guess it's true he could have been lying to us."

"*Jah*, we don't have any proof that Hazel was stealing. It could be a cover-up," Anna said. "I guess his motive could be that Hazel was breaking up with him?"

Beth nodded, "Now that you say that I wish we had asked him more questions."

Anna agreed, and wrote next to his name, *Hazel was breaking up with him.* "Ok, so last night, you and I were talking about the possibility that it could've been Peggy Fremont. I mean, she definitely has a motive."

"*Jah*, I agree. I don't think she did it, but we can't logically rule her out yet," Beth said. Her mind shifted again to Jonah. She wished she had visited with him last night and asked if he had any thoughts on all of this.

Anna wrote Peggy's name down and listed her motive as *Didn't get along with Hazel.*

"You can add that she also got a promotion after Hazel died. Maybe she wanted her job," Beth said.

Anna grimaced, "Ugh, that's two motives. I really hope it's not Peggy. Surely she wouldn't do something like that and risk leaving her daughters all alone."

"It's probably not her, but like you said, we have to look at everyone. Now let's think for a minute and see if there could be anyone else. Someone who might specifically want to frame Eva." Beth said.

The sisters looked at each other and said the name *Olivia Black* in unison.

"She certainly had something to gain from Eva's shop getting a bad reputation," Beth said as Anna scribbled Olivia's name on the paper.

Anna nodded as she wrote *Business competition* next to Olivia's name.

"Is there anyone we're not thinking of?" Anna asked.

Beth was quiet, and then she shook her head. "I can't think of anyone else. What about you?"

Anna shook her head. "No, I can't either. I think we should bring this list to Mark and Chris today and tell them about our conversation with Rick. They may want to go talk to him some more."

"*Jah*, we should do that, but can we please go check on Jonah first? I cannot stop worrying about him working there right next to two people that are on our suspect list," Beth said.

"Of course," Anna said. "Let's bring him some lunch, and maybe we can get him alone to ask him what he thinks."

Beth smiled at her sister, "*Denki, Schwester*. We'll go to the sheriff's office right after we stop by the inn."

The sisters packed up a turkey sandwich with a fresh tomato slice, some homemade chips, a handful of green grapes, and a couple sugar cookies in one of Eli's reusable cloth lunch bags for Jonah.

"I'll make sure Jonah gets the bag back to Eli," Beth assured her sister.

"Ah, I'm not worried about it. My husband has plenty of those bags. He wouldn't even know if one went missing," Anna said. "But, it might be a good excuse to have Jonah bring it back and stay for dinner sometime." She smiled and winked at Beth.

Beth grinned. "Once again, you and I are thinking the same thing, *Schwester*," she said.

Beth headed out the door ahead of Anna to pull the horse and buggy around the side of the house to the front.

Anna waited for her on the porch and then stepped up into her seat.

"Here we go again," Beth said, rolling her eyes as Anna reached for the handle. The two women laughed and headed toward the inn.

"This is becoming quite the well-traveled road for us, isn't it?" Anna asked, referring to their recent visits to the Amish Inn.

Beth nodded, keeping her eyes on the road. "*Jah*, I wonder if we'll see Sophia again today. I wouldn't mind it, if we did. I do enjoy her company."

"Oh, I feel the same way. She's very nice," Anna said. "We should give her a gift before she leaves."

"*Gut* idea!" Beth said. The sisters bounced gift ideas off of each other until they arrived at the Amish Inn.

They parked and immediately saw Jonah working out in the front yard with Sebastian. They had cleared all the dead vegetation and shrubbery and were leveling the ground, getting ready to plant new beautiful healthy plants in their place. A wheelbarrow holding potted new bushes and flowers sat just off to the side. Bags of mulch and pine bark lay on the ground next to the wheelbarrow.

"*Hallo*, Jonah and Sebastian!" Beth called out as she and Anna approached. Jonah and Sebastian stopped working and looked up, surprised to see the sisters. They waved and exchanged greetings.

"It's looking *wunderbaar* out here," Anna said, complimenting their work. "You have really turned this around."

"It's all him," Jonah said, pointing to Sebastian. "I'm just the helper, and only started that yesterday. Sebastian has been working very hard to clear all of this dead stuff out."

"Thank you," Sebastian said, "It's definitely comin' together." He leaned his hoe up against the wall of the inn and stretched his back. "This here kid is a wonderful help, I'll tell ya. You raised a good one, Mrs. Troyer." He patted Jonah on the back.

Jonah blushed and cast his eyes down to the ground.

"He has a lot of experience working outside with his Uncle Eli," Anna said, proudly.

"Well, he's fun to work with, *and* he's a hard worker. He definitely has a bright future ahead of him," Sebastian said. "Actually, it seems like success might just run in your family. I was just telling Jonah how much I love those butterscotch cream horns at your cousin's bakery. I get one every single mornin' on the way in to work."

"*Jah*, they are very good." Beth said. "We are certainly blessed to have so much talent in our family." She wanted to avoid talking about Eva, especially her cream horns, so she changed the subject. "Jonah, we brought you a lunch. Are you able to take a break while we're here?"

Jonah looked at Sebastian and he waved him away, "Go on. Take a break with your family. The work will still be here when you get done eatin' lunch."

"Thank you," Jonah mumbled as he set down his garden spade and walked toward his mother and aunt. "My water bottle is in the shed, I think. Want to follow me, and then we can sit at the picnic table on the back patio?"

The sisters nodded and Jonah led the way to the small outbuilding where the garden tools and supplies for the inn were kept.

"You'll have to take a peek and see how I organized the shed, *Maem* and Aunt Anna," Jonah said. "That project took me a few hours. Everything was just kinda thrown in there, but I attached hooks to the walls and tidied up."

As they approached, only one of the two side-by-side doors was open wide, so Jonah grabbed a hold of the handle on the other and pulled it open, displaying a very neatly organized tool and garden shed. A big smile spread across Beth's face as she immediately thought that the organizational skills reminded her of her husband, Jonah's father, Noah.

She opened her mouth to compliment Jonah when she stopped dead in her tracks. In the corner of her eye, she had spotted a large white five-gallon bucket sitting near the door. The word *Danger* was printed across the front and sides of the bucket in bright red, and just below the word was a picture of a skull and crossbones. A set of blue thick plastic gloves were placed on top of the sealed container.

Beth reached over and grabbed Anna's arm, pulling her close and whispering in her ear, "Look, Anna. Do you see that bucket over there with the blue gloves sitting on top?"

Anna looked where she was nodding her head and gasped.

"It looks good in here, don't it?" Sebastian's voice was loud and unexpected. Anna and Beth both jumped, and Beth squealed.

"*Ach du lieva*, you scared me!" Beth said as she turned around to see Sebastian standing in the doorway, blocking their exit. "Yes, we were just admiring Jonah's organizational work in here. It is very nice."

Sebastian stepped back as the women started to make their way out of the shed, Jonah following close behind with his water bottle.

"We're going to have a seat over there at the picnic table, if you would like to join us," Jonah said politely to Sebastian.

"Ah, no thanks, I was just comin' in here to grab a bigger shovel. Take your time and enjoy your meal with your family," Sebastian smiled.

Beth, Anna and Jonah started to walk toward the back patio when Beth stopped and turned around a moment later. "Hey, Sebastian," she called out.

"Yes?" Sebastian said, poking his head out of the shed.

"I noticed those blue gloves in there. Where did you get those? I haven't seen any plastic gloves that thick before, but I'd like to have something like that for home," she said.

Sebastian turned to look and said, "Oh, yeah, those are great. I actually found those at your family's hardware store."

Beth said, "Interesting. What did you use them for?"

Sebastian pushed his hands in his pockets and looked a little uncomfortable. "I used it when I had to handle pesticide. There were some pretty big critters around here that needed to be taken care of," he said.

# Chapter Fifteen

B eth and Anna sat with Jonah as he ate his lunch. Beth felt as if she might burst from sitting quietly across from Jonah making small talk. She held Anna's hand under the table, her knee bouncing. She wanted desperately to run off with Anna and go tell the sheriff everything, but she also didn't trust Sebastian with Jonah.

Her mind was racing.

When Sebastian made the remark about the critters, was he referring to Hazel, or was she imagining it?

She pictured the suspect list she had folded and tucked away in her apron pocket and wondered if they should add

Sebastian to the list. But what would be his motive? She couldn't find an answer in her head.

"*Maem*, are you even listening? You seem really distracted right now," Jonah said. "Everything ok?"

Jonah's voice snapped Beth out of her thoughts.

"*Jah*, I'm fine," Beth said. "I'm listening to you."

Anna squeezed Beth's hand and changed the subject before Jonah could test his mother's answer. "So, how are things since Hazel is gone?"

Jonah swallowed his last bite of sugar cookie and took a quick drink of water. "It's weird. There's a lot of tension in the air. It's almost like we shouldn't ever mention her name. Hank gets all weird about it. He must really miss her. I know she did a lot for him. I'm sure it must be an adjustment for him," Jonah rambled.

"How is Peggy doing?" Beth asked.

"She seems happier, which is to be expected. I mean, Hazel was really mean to Peggy all the time. I got the impression they knew each other from a long time ago and had some sort of bad history together." Jonah said. "Plus, it looks like Peggy may be taking over a lot of the responsibilities Hazel had. Hank said he's going to look to hire a new house cleaner."

"That's good news for Peggy, then," Beth said, trying hard to keep her voice flat.

"*Jah*, I think that it's *baremlich* what happened to Hazel, but there may be some good things that come out of it in the end," Jonah said.

Beth thought that Jonah sounded very optimistic. He had definitely made some positive changes since he started working at the inn. She and Noah were just talking the other night about how he was becoming quite the mature and responsible young man. They were both very proud.

"Well, I should get back to work, I guess. *Denki* for the delicious lunch," Jonah said. "I'll walk you to your buggy."

Beth rose quickly, anxious to get on the road and head toward the sheriff's office. She was glad to visit with Jonah, but there was so much to tell Mark and Chris that she couldn't help but feel antsy.

As the three of them approached the parking lot, they could see the sheriff's car parked next to her buggy.

"Mark and Chris are here," gasped Beth.

"Hmm, that's odd. I wonder why they're here," Jonah said innocently. "I hope everything is okay."

"Let's go in and see," said Anna. "We were supposed to meet with them today anyway. This will save us a trip."

"You two were supposed to meet with the sheriff today? What's going on here?" Jonah asked with a suspicious tone.

Beth sighed and hooked one arm through Jonah's and the other arm through Anna's, and walking towards the front door of the inn, she said, "Oh, Jonah. You *know* why we're supposed to go see the sheriff."

Jonah rolled his eyes. "Don't tell me you two are doing some kind of investigation into Hazel's murder. Does Dad and Uncle Eli know about this?" Jonah asked, but the question remained unanswered as the three of them opened the door and stepped inside.

They could hear Hank's voice, tense and loud coming from the dining area.

"Nobody here had anything to do with Hazel's death, Sheriff," Hank said.

The sheriff responded in a normal, calm tone, but the sisters couldn't decipher what he was saying. Entering the dining room, Beth dropped her arms down by her side, releasing her sister and her son from her grip. They had just walked into what appeared to be a staff meeting, minus Jonah - and with Sheriff Streen and Deputy Jones.

Peggy was crying on Emily's shoulder off to the side of the room. Hank was red in the face standing across from Mark and Chris. Sebastian stood tall next to Hank as if he were literally on Hank's side.

When the men saw Anna, Beth and Jonah enter the room, Hank pointed and said loudly, "Ask them! They went to go visit Hazel's boyfriend. Tell them, ladies. Tell them what Rick said. *He* should be the one you're questioning. Not disrupting *our* day here when we're trying to work."

Mark and Chris turned to look at Anna and Beth. Jonah stepped aside. He looked like he wanted to dig a hole in the floor and hide. He just remained quiet standing a couple feet away from his mother and aunt.

Mark and Chris approached the sisters and Mark said in a low voice with his back to the rest of the room, "Hello, ladies. We saw your buggy out there and were wondering when you were gonna show up." He smiled.

All eyes were on Beth and Anna. Anna whispered to the sheriff, "We've got something to tell you, but it's not about Rick."

"Speak up, ladies," Hank said in a boisterous tone. "You might as well get it all out in the open. Tell us what you found out about Rick. We're all waiting."

Mark and Chris turned back around and moved out of the way. All eyes were on Anna and Beth. Beth's hands were clasped together in front of her, and she worked very hard to remain still and hide that she was trembling.

Anna spoke in a clear voice, "Well, Hank, it's true that we went to visit Rick." She turned to the sheriff and deputy and said, "Rick Storm was Hazel's boyfriend. They had been fighting and Hazel had wanted him to move out."

Hank interrupted, "Ah, that's why she wanted to stay in a room here for a few nights. That makes sense." Then, after a brief pause, he said, "Go on... for Pete's sake, what did Rick say?"

Anna looked at Beth, and Beth nodded for Anna to continue. She had so much to say herself, but she worried that her voice would sound shaky.

Anna continued, "Rick said that Hazel was stealing a lot of money from Hank."

It was like a bomb had hit the room. Hank, Sebastian and Emily gasped loudly.

Peggy spoke up, "It's true. Hazel *was* stealing from Hank. She was taking money from all the cash receipts. I saw her do it once, and she threatened that if I ever told, she would blame me and I would lose my job. I'm so sorry, Hank. I couldn't say anything. She was going to pin it all on me." Her voice cracked and tears started to stream down her cheeks again. Emily put an arm around her shoulders for comfort.

Mark looked at Hank. "So, this is an interesting discovery, Hank," he said.

Chris agreed, "It does look like a pretty tight motive. That, along with the murder happening right here at your inn..."

Hank's face turned a darker red and his fists were clenched by his side, "I didn't know anything about this!" He yelled, and spit flew out of his mouth into the air. "I didn't know she was stealing from me! Ask Sebastian. He'll tell ya."

Sebastian stood there, still as a rock.

Mark and Chris weren't believing it. "I think you should come down to the station with us, Hank, give us some fingerprints and answer a few more questions."

Hank was speechless. His mouth dropped open. Beth felt sorry for him. She believed he didn't do it, and she was afraid he might be blamed.

"But my fingerprints are everywhere here. I mean, this is my business," Hank's voice had dropped to a normal level. He was begging for Mark and Chris to believe his innocence.

Mark spoke with a stern voice. His patience was running thin, and he said to Hank, "Look, you can either come voluntarily or we can break out the handcuffs and take you out, risking that the reporter is around with her camera."

Mark took a step forward, but he was interrupted when Beth let out a squeak.

"Wait," Beth said, her voice sounding timid and forced. "There's something else," she managed to say.

Everyone stopped and the room got quiet. Hank sent her a look of gratitude.

Beth cleared her throat before continuing. "Hank may have the motive," she said, "but you could argue that Peggy does, too."

Peggy gasped and let out a cry.

"What I mean is," Beth's voice got louder, "that we're missing one of the most important things here."

Everyone looked at Beth in anticipation.

"The murder weapon," she said, and she looked directly at Sebastian.

# Chapter Sixteen

---

Sebastian looked at Hank. Beth thought that his eyes showed a mixture of fear and regret. The room was silent in response to Beth's mention of a murder weapon.

Mark spoke, "Beth, I'm not sure what you're getting at. The murder weapon was the pastry, was it not?"

Chris said, "I see what you're getting at, Beth. Maybe it doesn't make sense that Hank would purchase a pastry from Sugar on Top to kill Hazel."

Beth nodded. She was hoping Sebastian would speak up because even she wasn't sure he was the killer. She had him with the murder weapon but not the motive. He was in an exact opposite position that she had put Hank in. Her mind was spinning. Now, she wondered if it might be Peggy after all. Peggy had the motive *and* she had access to all the pastries at the bakery. Beth instantly regretted speaking up and was more confused than before.

Anna jumped in, "Sheriff Streen and Deputy Jones, can you please tell us what flavor cream horn was found, poisoned, next to Hazel's bed?"

The deputy looked confused.

Beth thought she saw Sebastian start to fidget.

Deputy Chris Jones looked at his mentor, and after receiving a nod from the sheriff, he said, "It was butterscotch flavored."

Anna and Beth glanced at each other again. That was it!

Jonah spoke up, "Sebastian, didn't you say that you bought a butterscotch cream horn every day from Sugar on Top?

Sebastian didn't answer. He was clearly getting more and more uncomfortable with the direction this conversation was going.

Beth was next, "And is it just a coincidence that the pesticide in the five gallon bucket out there in the corner of the shed is a poisonous white powder? With the similar appearance of confectioners' sugar?"

That's all the sheriff and deputy needed to hear. They grabbed Sebastian and put his hands behind his back, quickly clicking the handcuffs in place and reading him his Miranda rights.

Sebastian didn't put up a fight. He stood there, his head hung low.

Hank asked the sheriff if he could wait just one moment before escorting Sebastian to their car, and the sheriff agreed.

"Why did you do it, Sebastian? You had so much going for you," Hank asked with a kind voice.

Sebastian lifted his face and made eye contact with Hank. He paused for a few seconds, leaving doubt as to if he would even respond. Then quietly, he said, "I did it for you. What she was doin' to you wasn't right, Hank. And she wasn't just doin' it to you. At the rate she was goin', everyone here was going to lose their jobs. Not only was she stealin' from you, Hank, but she was stealin' from all of us."

He paused again before he continued. "I know you liked her. At one point, I thought you probably kept givin' her chances like you gave me a chance. But I couldn't sit back and keep watchin' it and waitin' for the worst to happen. These people are good people you have workin' for you, Hank. None of y'all deserve to be treated like that."

Beth's heart melted as she realized Sebastian's motive was based on good intentions.

Hank patted his back, and Sebastian continued. "I said it before, Hank, and I'll say it again. I thank ya for allowin' me to be a part of this here group of people, even if it was for a short time. I'll never forget it," he leaned forward and whispered to Hank, "and I'd do it all the same if I had to do it over."

The deputy asked, "So, did you have this whole thing planned out?" He hoped the answer was no, so he could possibly get a lighter sentence.

Sebastian shook his head, "No, I actually didn't. I had to go pick up that pesticide for the field mice that I found running around outside and the clerk warned me of how dangerous the stuff could be if it were ingested. That same day, I overheard Hazel tell Peggy that she needed the yella room cleaned because she was stayin' there for a few nights. That's when I had the idea, and it all came together in my head when I purchased the cream horn and saw the powdered sugar on top. It all came together so easy, that it was almost meant to happen. She was so greedy that she didn't even suspect anything when I offered her my cream horn."

Then Sebastian looked over where Jonah and the sisters stood and said, "I'm real sorry about the trouble that came with using that pastry. I didn't think that one through."

The sisters thanked him. Anna said, "You are a very brave and good-hearted man. We will pray for *Gotte* to forgive you for your sins, and you should do the same."

Beth added, "Yes, and there is an Amish proverb that I hope you'll remember. It says, 'You appreciate the light much more once you have come through the darkness.' May *Gotte* bless you, Sebastian."

All eyes in the room watched as the sheriff and deputy led Sebastian out to their car. Anna and Beth said good-bye to Jonah and the rest of the crew at the Amish Inn. Heading down the front porch steps, they saw the sheriff and deputy pulling out of the parking lot. Sheriff Streen stopped the car and rolled down his window.

"Well, you two did it again," he said with a smile from ear to ear. "I can't thank you enough for all your help."

Deputy Jones leaned forward and said, "Your detective skills are truly impressive! Maybe the two of you should start a private investigator business."

Beth looked at Anna, her eyes wide and a big grin on her face.

Anna looked at Beth and then back at the men sitting in the car, and said, "Oh, no. Don't even get her started." She rolled her eyes and grabbed her sister's hand, pulling her toward the buggy.

"Let's go home. That's enough excitement for the day," she said.

"Bye, ladies! See you at the market on Saturday!" Sheriff Mark Streen called out as he pulled away.

The women waved goodbye and climbed into Beth's buggy. Anna grabbed hold of the handle, and the two women looked at each other and smiled. No words were necessary.

# Chapter Seventeen

———◦◆◦———

B eth drummed her pencil on the table, the list of items needed for the Schwartz's homecoming party sat in front of her, words marked out in several places.

"I just really want it to be so special," Beth said quietly.

Noah reached over and grabbed another spoonful of his favorite breakfast casserole. "The parties you plan with your sister are always perfect," he said, as he pushed his fork into a clump of cheesy goodness. "And there's always more than enough *wunderbaar* food."

"*Denki*, my *lieb*," Beth said with a warm smile. She and Noah had grown up together and married at a young age.

After a wonderful life of raising children, she was still as happy as the day they met.

"Oh, before I forget," Beth said, "Could I please have one of the horse and buggy figurines out of the few you have in your shop?" Noah was a talented woodworker, and his small hand-carved figurines were popular items at the market. The horse and buggy figure was Beth's favorite, and she wanted to give it to Sophia as a souvenir.

Noah nodded, "Of course. I just carved a few new ones yesterday, so your timing is perfect."

"*Wunderbaar*!" Beth said. "I'll grab one this morning, then."

As Beth stood to clear the table, there was a soft knock as the back door opened slowly.

"*Gute mariye!*" Anna called cheerily, as she let herself inside.

"*Gute mariye, Schwester!*" Beth said, setting her freshly washed plate on a dish towel laid out next to the sink. Noah, with his mouth full, nodded and waved.

"How's the list coming along, Beth?" Anna said, reaching for the bowl of fruit on the table and carrying it to the counter. Beth thanked her and snapped a lid on top of the bowl.

"It's *gut*," Beth said, "I think we have everything we need, but I would love your eyes on it, of course."

Anna grabbed a coffee mug from the cabinet and poured herself a cup of fresh coffee from the half empty pour-over carafe sitting on the table. She sat down at the end of the table and took a sip. "Mmmmm," she said, "Beth, your coffee is always so yummy."

"How's Eli this morning?" Noah asked Beth before rising to his feet and carrying his dish to the sink.

"Oh, he's very busy these days. Harvesting and planning for the Fall season. It will be here before we know it." Anna said, and Noah nodded in agreement.

"I look forward to hearing how the farm is doing at the Schwartz's party," Noah said before turning to his wife. "*Denki*, Beth for the delicious breakfast. I'm headed out to help Jacob today," he said. He walked over to the bench by the door and sat down to slip on his shoes.

Beth nodded. "Have a blessed day, dear," she said as she settled down across the table from Anna, list in hand.

"Ok, let's see what we've got," Anna said, and the twins dove into planning mode. Noah placed his hat on his head and snuck out the back door unnoticed.

After determining their grocery list and their plan of attack for the preparation, the sisters topped off their coffee cups with the last of the coffee, leaning back in their seats at the same time.

"I'm excited to see Sophia today," Beth said.

Anna nodded, "*Jah*, me too. It's sad to see her go. I hope she'll consider returning for a visit some time."

Beth swallowed her coffee and said, "I wonder what things are like at the inn this morning."

"Well, I guess we can ask Sophia," Anna said, pointing to the picture window behind Beth's seat at the table. A car had pulled up, and Sophia stepped out.

Beth turned and smiled, "Oh, *gut!* She's early!" The sisters stood, smoothed out their aprons, and tucked imaginary loose strands of hair into their *kapps*.

Beth opened the door just as Sophia's feet touched the front porch. "Welcome!" She said with a broad smile on her face.

"*Gut mariye!*" Sophia said to both the sisters, and Anna suggested they have a seat in the front living room.

Beth excused herself for a moment to step out back and gather the wooden horse and buggy figurine that she wanted to give to Sophia and returned to find that Anna had set a kettle of water on the stove for tea.

"So, I'm dying to hear all about it!" Sophia sat on the edge of the couch, leaning forward. "I could barely sleep all night. If you had a phone, I would've surely called you. I passed the sheriff's car on the way home and I could see poor Sebastian seated in the back. Of course, I didn't feel comfortable asking anyone at the inn for more information."

"It was just *baremlich*," said Anna, shaking her head. "It was indeed Sebastian who killed Hazel."

Beth chimed in, "*Jah*, he confessed to everyone."

Beth and Anna took turns replaying the scene at the inn where everything unfolded, as Sophia sat in awe.

"Oh, I'm so sad that this whole thing happened. Sebastian really came across as a nice person, and he and Jonah seemed close. As a matter of fact, all the crew at the inn appeared to be pretty tight knit," Sophia remarked.

"*Jah*, everyone except for Hazel, I guess," Beth muttered.

"I guess you're right about that," said Sophia. "So, in the end, Sebastian poisoned Hazel because she was stealing from Hank?"

Anna nodded. "*Jah*, and I guess he thought he was protecting everyone. He was worried that they would all lose their jobs. At the rate she was stealing, the inn wouldn't have lasted long."

Beth agreed. "I guess you could say he had good intentions, but sometimes even good intentions can lead you down the wrong path."

Sophia and Anna nodded.

"Yes, if there is a lesson here, I would say that's it," Anna said.

The kettle on the stove whistled, and Beth stood to prepare some tea for the three of them. Inviting Sophia and Anna to sit at the table, she set out homemade bread and jam and filled their cups. She grabbed the figurine off the kitchen counter and placed it next to Sophia's plate.

"A small token of our appreciation for your help solving this crime, Sophia," Beth said.

Sophia squealed and grabbed it, holding it up to admire the hand carving. "Oh, it's beautiful! *Denki*, Beth!"

"*Denki* to you, Sophia, for visiting Little Valley," Anna said with a warm smile. "We hope you'll come back to visit us soon."

"Of course, I will," Sophia said. "I have fallen in love with this beautiful little town and the wonderful people here. I have really enjoyed my stay."

"How is the article coming along?" Beth asked.

"Oh, I've just barely started writing the final draft," Sophia replied, "but, I promise to leave Hazel's story out of it! I can write about Heaven's Diner, and Main Street, and our ride in your buggy." She smiled and held up the figurine. "I have some wonderful pictures of the inn, too, but it feels like I'm still missing something. I've extended my flight home an extra day to see if I can do a bit more exploration and meet a few more people."

Anna looked at Beth and said, "I just had a really *gut* idea, I think."

Beth grinned and nodded, "I think I know what you're going to say, and I think it's a very *gut* idea indeed."

"Would you like to join us for a gathering in the community tomorrow? Our friends have adopted a new baby. It is a joyous moment for all of us, and we would love to introduce you to everyone." Anna said, her eyes shining.

"Yes! I would love that!" Sophia bounced in her seat and clasped her hands in front of her. "As long as it's ok with the family, of course..."

"If there's one thing, you'll learn about our community is that our welcoming arms stretch wide. It's a *wunderbaar* idea. We'll see you back here tomorrow. Don't eat too much beforehand!"

The women finished their tea, laughing together and comparing life in the big city with that of one spent in a small town. At some point while Anna and Sophia chatted, Beth became silent to just sit, be present and appreciate the moment. Her life was full of love and happiness, and her heart was full of gratitude.

# Chapter Eighteen

---

"He's so perfect!" Beth exclaimed, holding Rachel's brand-new baby, Jeremiah, in her arms.

"Isn't he just *wunderbaar*?" Rachel replied, her face beaming with pride.

"How is he sleeping?" Abigail asked, and before Rachel could answer, Mary chimed in, "Is he eating well?"

Rachel laughed and answered, "He truly is such a *gut* baby. He's been home for a little over a week now and he is sleeping through the night. And he eats like a growing boy."

Anna leaned in their conversation, "Did you ladies get some food? Beth worked really hard on all the planning and preparations, and we don't want anything to go to waste."

Beth smiled and said, "Oh, everyone knows it wasn't just me." She winked at Anna. "But *jah*, please do eat!"

Sarah showed up next to Anna and nudged her arm. "Look, *Maem*, there's a car outside."

The ladies looked out the picture window and saw Sophia stepping out of a drive share vehicle. She was wearing a smart yellow dress with white dress flats. Her hair was tied back on one side.

"It's Sophia," Beth said.

"Oh, good! I'm looking forward to meeting the famous reporter in town," Sarah said over her shoulder as she headed towards the door. She swung the door open wide with a warm smile on her face.

"*Gut daag*," Sophia said, smiling back.

"Welcome!" Sarah waved Sophia in and shut the door behind her.

"I'm so glad you made it," said Beth. "I was starting to wonder if you had to head back early."

Sophia blushed. "I am notoriously late for things for which I choose to wear something nicer than jeans and tennis shoes. I'm so sorry I'm late."

Anna waved her hand in the air, "Oh, it's fine. This isn't that formal and you didn't miss much."

Sophia suddenly caught a glimpse of baby Jeremiah. "Oooh, this must be the man of the hour," she said, cocking her head. "He's beautiful!"

"*Denki*," Rachel said.

"You must be Rachel, the lucky *maem*. It's a pleasure to meet you; I've heard wonderful things about you and your family." Sophia said.

Rachel smiled shyly and said, "Likewise."

"Wait, don't tell me. It's clear that the two of you," Sophia said, pointing to both Abigail and Sarah, "are related to these two women." She paused briefly before continuing. "But, there's no way I'm going to be able to tell who belongs to whom." Her comment was met with friendly giggles, as a crowd had started to create a circle around Sophia and the twins.

Anna and Beth went around the room introducing all the ladies to Sophia, sharing bits of stories here and there, and baby Jeremiah was passed around or just cooed over by each person. Questions were asked and advice was shared, and the food at the table began to disappear.

A few hours later, the crowd had started to disperse, and the time had come for Sophia to say goodbye, as well.

"I promise to keep in touch," Sophia said as she embraced Anna and Beth in one big hug.

"And please visit," Beth said, and Anna nodded.

"Oh, I will! Don't worry!" Sophia stepped into the backseat of the ride share car she had ordered and rolled down the window.

"*Denki*, Anna and Beth. For everything! It was so wonderful to meet you both!" Sophia said, as the car started to inch forward.

"Be safe!" Anna called out as the car drove away.

"I'm so glad she was able to make it," Anna said to Beth.

"Oh, me, too. Everyone just loved her," Beth replied, linking her arm in Anna's and leading her back to the house. "Now, we have a house to clean!"

"We sure do!" Anna said, as she patted her sister's hand. "Great party, *Schwester*," she said with a grin.

"We did it again, *Schwester*,' Beth grinned back and winked.

---

In the next story of the Amish Lantern Mystery Series, Jessica McLean opens shop to find a man has been left for dead on the floor of her diner. With very few clues left behind, Jessica becomes the prime murder suspect. But Beth and Anna wonder if the crime could be related to Jessica's new relationship with their beloved Matthew. It soon becomes clear that things aren't always as they seem, and the sisters step in to try to solve the mystery and bring justice to Little Valley yet again.

A Blessing in Disguise is the fifth (and next!) book in the Amish Lantern Mystery Series. Visit my website at **marybbarbee.com** to grab your copy!

---

Is your mouth watering after reading all about those delicious Amish treats? Well, I have a gift for you! Visit **marybbarbee.com/ALMS-cookbook** to get instant access to Anna and Beth's family secret Amish Sugar Cookies... and so much more, including a few extra mouth-watering recipes that are introduced later in the Amish Lantern Mystery Series.

# *Acknowledgments*

---

I love this part of my books because I get to take a few minutes to thank everyone in my life who has made The Amish Lantern Mystery Series a successful reality. Trust me when I say that it is so much more than just my writing.

I will start with graciously thanking my loyal readers. It is because of your dedication and love that I am encouraged to continue creating more stories about Anna and Beth, and the dozens of other characters in Little Valley. When I see how many people across the globe are enjoying my books, I am moved. There is simply no other word to describe it. So, thank you. Thank you for being patient with me as I sometimes take too long to write the next book. Thank you for your comments and reviews (yes, even lower rated reviews are appreciated!). And thank you for the emails! I truly adore hearing from all of you.

Thank you to my editors and beta readers for such a wonderful job, reminding me of things like the word community is plural, not singular, even though I am talking about a group of people. And thank you even more for providing such incredible insight into how the world inside my books can look different to readers (versus what lives inside my mind). Thank you for all your hard work turning what I've written into something even better.

Thank you to my closest family and friends for understanding when I spent hours upon hours "in Little Valley" finishing this book - and not holding it against me when it takes me a while to return a phone call or a text message. Thank you for your patience when the book is all I talk about, and when I seem "out of it" at dinner or am ready for bed before the sun sets. I know how much you love and support me in this journey, and I'm beyond grateful for all of it.

In the previous book, I ended the Acknowledgements page with *Denki*, and it's so fitting, I have decided to make that a tradition. So...

As the Amish say beautifully, *Denki*. I am forever grateful.

# A Note From the Author

---

Thank you for reading *Good Intentions*. On one hand, I can't believe this is already the fourth book in *The Amish Lantern Mystery Series*, but on the other hand, it feels like I've "lived" in Little Valley for years and years.

As I was writing this story, I found myself writing much longer chapters than in the other books, and at some point, I thought this novella was going to graduate into a novel. I worried about that, although briefly, since I know most of my readers are looking for that shorter style, but somehow it packaged together perfectly to be about the same length as the others – just with less chapters. I still can't figure that one out, but I didn't question it. Honestly, a lot of the time, I feel like the book writes itself and I'm just the vessel that does the typing.

A few tears dropped writing Chapter 16. I hate to see good people punished for their mistakes, but I designed the plot, and I was too far in to change things by that point. And despite those feelings, I do believe that *Good Intentions* is now my new favorite.

I also really enjoyed creating Sophia's character. The thought of a journalist working for a faith tourism magazine was so intriguing that I decided to write a spin-off mystery series to run alongside *The Amish Lantern Mystery Series*, with the same name as the magazine: *Faith Afar*.

Overall, it feels wonderful to share the story of Good Intentions with the world! I hope you enjoyed reading it as much as I enjoyed writing it!

If you want to read more about the wonderful citizens in Little Valley or find out where Sophia Adams's next assignment is, you can sign up on my website at maryb barbee.com for my new release newsletter.

Want to follow me on social media? Follow me on Facebook and Instagram.

I'm also on Goodreads and on Bookbub, too.

Thank you again for choosing *Good Intentions* to add to your book selection. Please consider leaving a review or recommending it to a friend!

With so much gratitude,

Mary B.

# About the Author

Mary B. Barbee is the author of the *Amish Lantern Mystery Series*. As an avid fan of all mystery and suspense in print, on television and in film, Mary B. believes the best mystery is one where the suspect changes throughout the story, keeping the audience guessing. She enjoys providing an exciting escape for a few hours with stories her readers can't put down - and always with a surprise ending.

When not writing, Mary B. is either playing a couple sets of tennis or a strategy board game with her two witty daughters and her kindly competitive mother. The four of them share a home in the Inland Northwest in the beautiful town of Spokane, Washington with their really cute - but sometimes naughty - chihuahua.

Mary B. loves to hear from her readers. Connect at:

marybbarbee@gmail.com

www.facebook.com/marybbarbee

Instagram @marybbarbee

www.marybbarbee.com

# More Books to Read By Mary B. Barbee

---

**THE AMISH LANTERN MYSTERY SERIES**

*Thick As Thieves – Book 1*

Robberies are running rampant in Little Valley, and the quiet small-town lives of the Amish community are suddenly thrown into chaos.

### Secrets in Little Valley – Book 2
With the bishop's daughter suddenly missing and a new sheriff in town, Anna and Beth find themselves roped into solving another mystery in their small town.

### Saving Grace – Book 3
The Amish community in Little Valley is facing big changes, and big threats, with tourism booming. It becomes clear that some of the new businesses want control of the market, and it looks like they are willing to go to great lengths to get it.

### Good Intentions – Book 4
Hazel Thompson is found dead in Little Valley's now-famous Amish Inn, and there's a long list of suspects with plenty of motive.

### A Blessing in Disguise – Book 5
Jessica McLean opens shop to find a man has been left for dead on the floor of her diner. Could the crime could be related to Jessica's new relationship with their beloved Matthew Beiler?

### Christmas Chaos in Little Valley - Book 6

Beth finds out that the Little Valley library is shutting its doors due to a lack of funding and very disturbing anonymous threats.

———◆◇◆———

## THE ABIGAIL BAKER MYSTERY SERIES
### *Blind Faith – Prequel*

Abigail's excitement for her new home is replaced by doom and gloom when she finds out that an unexplained murder has rocked the residents of her new town. And not unusual to her, it's the Amish community that is suspect number one.

**Grab your free e-copy of Blind Faith at:**
**marybbarbee.com/blindfaith**

### *Where Fear Ends – Book 1*

A town councilman is found dead by the side of the road in the Amish community of Abigail Baker's new hometown.

### *A Multitude of Sins – Book 2*

When secret notes containing serious threats are unveiled, Abigail wonders if the latest victim could have been hiding a multitude of sins.

*A Wing and a Prayer – Book 3  ~ COMING SOON!*

---

## THE PUPCAKE MYSTERY SERIES
### *Cupcakes and Corruption – Prequel*

Battling empty-nest syndrome, Eliza finds solace in the company of her adorable chihuahua, Pupcake, and her dreams of opening a quaint coffee shop. Little does she know that her talent for baking and nurturing also extends to amateur sleuthing.

**Grab your free e-copy of Cupcakes and Corruption at:**
**marybbarbee.com/pupcakeprequel**

### *Sweet Suspicion – Book 1*

The charming town of Copeland is buzzing with excitement as Eliza and her adorable chihuahua, Pupcake, open their new coffee shop. But when a body is discovered on the premises, the duo must put down their baking tools and pick up their detective hats.

### *Confections and Clues – Book 2 – Coming Valentine's Day 2025*

Eliza and Pupcake's lakeside getaway takes a dark turn when they stumble upon a body. With a secretive small town and a case no one wants solved, Eliza's sweet retreat quickly turns into another mystery. Can she and Pupcake crack the case before the killer's trail goes cold?

### *Recipe for Reckoning – Book 3 ~ COMING SOON!*

---

Find excerpts, purchase links and more at
www.marybbarbee.com